# George Peele's The Arraignment of Paris: A Retelling

David Bruce

Published by David Bruce, 2022.

GEORGE PEELE'S THE ARRAIGNMENT OF PARIS: A RETELLING

First edition. July 20, 2022.

Copyright © 2022 David Bruce.

ISBN: 979-8201550431

Written by David Bruce.

# Table of Contents

# Dedication

Dedicated to Carl Eugene Bruce and Josephine Saturday Bruce

My father, Carl Eugene Bruce, died on 24 October 2013. He used to work for Ohio Power, and at one time, his job was to shut off the electricity of people who had not paid their bills. He sometimes would find a home with an impoverished mother and some children. Instead of shutting off their electricity, he would tell the mother that she needed to pay her bill or soon her electricity would be shut off. He would write on a form that no one was home when he stopped by because if no one was home he did not have to shut off their electricity.

The best good deed that anyone ever did for my father occurred after a storm that knocked down many power lines. He and other linemen worked long hours and got wet and cold. Their feet were freezing because water got into their boots and soaked their socks. Fortunately, a kind woman gave my father and the other linemen dry socks to wear.

My mother, Josephine Saturday Bruce, died on 14 June 2003. She used to work at a store that sold clothing. One day, an impoverished mother with a baby clothed in rags walked into the store and started shoplifting in an interesting way: The mother took the rags off her baby and dressed the infant in new clothing. My mother knew that this mother could not afford to buy the clothing, but she helped the mother dress her baby and then she watched as the mother walked out of the store without paying.

My mother and my father both died at 7:40 p.m.

Cover Photograph for George Peele's *The Arraignment of Paris*: A Retelling:

Claudio_Scott

https://pixabay.com/photos/girl-women-beauty-costume-apple-2211717/

Note: A losing goddess is not amused by Venus' flaunting of the apple that is the prize for winning the beauty contest.

Educate Yourself
Read Like A Wolf Eats
Be Excellent to Each Other
Books Then, Books Now, Books Forever

****

In this retelling, as in all my retellings, I have tried to make the work of literature accessible to modern readers who may lack some of the the knowledge about mythology, religion, and history that the literary work's contemporary audience had.

Do you know a language other than English? If you do, I give you permission to translate this book, copyright your translation, publish or self-publish it, and keep all the royalties for yourself. (Do give me credit, of course, for the original retelling.)

I would like to see my retellings of classic literature used in schools, so I give permission to the country of Finland (and all other countries) to give copies of this book to all students forever. I also give permission to the state of Texas (and all other states) to give copies of this book to all students forever. I also give permission to all teachers to give copies of this book to all students forever.

Teachers need not actually teach my retellings. Teachers are welcome to give students copies of my books as background material. For example, if they are teaching Homer's *Iliad* and *Odyssey*, teachers are welcome to give students copies of my *Virgil's Aeneid: A Retelling in Prose* and tell students, "Here's another ancient epic you may want to read in your spare time."

# CAST OF CHARACTERS

**The Olympian Gods and Goddesses**

*Jupiter,* king of all the gods. He is often called Jove.

*Juno,* queen of the gods.

*Apollo,* god of music, medicine, and the Sun.

*Bacchus,* god of wine and revelry.

*Diana,* goddess of hunting and chastity. An alternate name for Diana is Phoebe.

*Mars,* god of war.

*Mercury,* Jupiter's messenger.

*Neptune,* ruler of the seas.

*Pallas,* goddess of war and wisdom. Pallas is Pallas Athena, whose Roman name is Minerva.

*Pluto,* ruler of the underworld: the Land of the Dead. Pluto is also known as Dis.

*Venus,* goddess of beauty and sexual passion.

*Vulcan,* the blacksmith god.

**Minor Gods and Goddesses**

*Pan,* god of flocks and herdsman.

*Faunus,* god of fields.

*Silvanus,* god of forests.

*Saturn,* god of agriculture.

*Pomona,* goddess of orchards and gardens.

*Flora,* goddess of flowers and gardens.

*Até,* goddess of discord.

*Clotho,* one of the Fates. She spins the thread of life.

*Lachesis,* one of the Fates. She measures the thread of life.

*Atropos,* one of the Fates. She cuts the thread of life. When a person's thread of life is cut, the person dies.

*The Muses,* protectors of the arts.

A *Nymph* of Diana.

*Rhanis,* a nymph.

Mortals

*Paris,* a shepherd, son of King Priam of Troy.

*Colin,* a shepherd.

*Hobbinol,* a shepherd.

*Diggon,* a shepherd.

*Thenot,* a shepherd.

*Oenone,* a nymph, at one time beloved by Paris.

*Helen,* wife of King Menelaus of Sparta. The most beautiful woman in the world.

*Thestylis,* a mortal woman beloved by Colin.

Cupids, Cyclopes (plural), Shepherds, Knights, etc.

Setting

The valleys and woods of Mount Ida, near Troy, in Asia Minor.

Notes

See Appendix A for Background Information about the Judgment of Paris and the Trojan War. That background knowledge is necessary for understanding this book.

In this culture, the word "wench" was not necessarily used negatively. It was often used affectionately.

A nymph is a nature spirit who looks like a beautiful young woman. They live in natural settings such as woods.

In George Peele's play, Até is confused with her mother, Eris, the goddess of strife. It was Eris who brought the golden ball (aka the golden apple) to the wedding of the mortal Peleus and the nymph Thetis, parents of Achilles, and caused strife.

The cover photograph shows a red apple, but Até's apple was golden.

George Peele's play concerns the Judgment of Paris, in which Paris, Prince of Troy, judges a beauty contest among three goddesses: Venus, Juno, and Pallas. He choses Venus, causing Juno and Pallas to accuse

2

him of bias, an accusation that leads to him being put on trial and judged by some male gods.

After the play concludes, Paris travels to Sparta, from which he runs away with Helen, the most beautiful woman in the world. She, of course, becomes known as Helen of Troy.

Check out Peter Lukac's excellent elizabethandrama.org edition of the play here:

https://tinyurl.com/yxbnd37g

# PROLOGUE

Até, the goddess of discord, speaks now to you, the reader of this book. Consistent with her character, she regards you as a damned soul:

"Condemned soul, from lowest hell and the deadly rivers of the infernal Jove — Pluto, ruler of the Land of the Dead — where bloodless ghostly souls in pains of endless duration fill ruthless, pitiless ears with never-ceasing cries, behold, I, Até, have come to this place, and I bring in addition the bane of Troy!"

She held up a golden apple and said, "Behold, the fruit of fate, torn from the golden tree of Proserpine, goddess of vegetation!

"Proud Troy must fall, so the gods above have ordered, and stately Ilium's lofty towers must be razed and torn down by the conquering hands of the victorious foe."

Ilium is another name for Troy.

Até continued, "And King Priam's younger son, the shepherd youth, Paris, the unhappy organ of the Greeks, must die."

Paris, Prince of Troy, is the organ or agent of the Greeks in that he is the reason the Greeks will make war against the Trojans.

"King Priam's Trojan palace must be laid waste with flaming fire, whose thick and foggy smoke, piercing the sky, must serve as the messenger of sacrifice, to appease the anger of the angry heavens.

"When the gods on Mount Olympus see the smoke of burning Troy, they will know that what was fated to happen has been accomplished.

"So, averse to and weary of her heavy load, and surcharged with the burden that she will no longer sustain, the Earth complains to Pluto, ruler of the hellish Land of the Dead.

"So many dead will lie on the plains of Troy that the Earth will complain to Pluto, who will then receive the dead's ghostly souls into the Land of the Dead.

"The three Fates, who are impartial daughters of Ananke, goddess of Necessity, will be her aides in her petition complaining about the deaths of so many people in such a short period of time during the fall of Troy.

"And so the twine that holds old Priam's house, the thread of Troy, Dame Atropos with her knife cuts asunder."

The three Fates commanded the pulse of life; they controlled human life. Clotho spun the thread of life. Lachesis measured the thread of life, determining how long a person lived. Atropos cut the thread of life; when the thread was cut, the person died.

Até continued, "Done must be the pleasure of the powers above, whose commands men must obey, and I must perform my part in the valleys around Mount Ida.

"Lordings, adieu. Imposing silence for your task, I end my speech, until the just assembly of the goddesses makes me begin the tragedy of Troy."

Até exited with the golden apple.

# CHAPTER 1

— 1.1 —

Pan, Faunus, and Silvanus, with their attendants — a shepherd, a hunter, and a woodman — stood and talked together.

Pan's shepherd had a lamb, Faunus' hunter had a fawn, and Silvanus' woodman had an oak bough laden with acorns. The animals and the oak branch laden with acorns were gifts.

All of them were here to welcome three goddesses who were expected to appear soon: Juno, Pallas, and Venus.

Pan, Faunus, and Silvanus, however, were afraid that they had arrived later than they ought to in order to greet the goddesses. Pan was afraid that either Flora, the goddess of flowers and gardens, or Faunus had made them arrive late.

"Silvanus, either Flora does us wrong, or Faunus made us tarry all too long, for by this morning mirth it would appear that the Muses or the three goddesses are near," Pan said.

The Muses are goddesses of the arts.

"My fawn was nimble, Pan, and dashed madly about," Faunus said. "Happily we caught him up at last — he is the fattest, fairest fawn in all the woods where game animals live. I wonder how the knave could skip so fast."

"And I have brought a twagger — a fat lamb — for the occasion, a bunting — plump — lamb," Pan said. "Please, touch it — you will feel no bones. Believe me now that I am much mistaken if ever Pan has felt a fatter lamb than this."

One characteristic of these gods (and the goddesses) is that they often spoke of themselves in the third person.

Silvanus said, "Sirs, you may boast about your flocks and herds that are both fresh and fair, yet Silvanus has walks in the woods, truly, that stand in wholesome air, and, look, the honor of the woods, the gallant

6

oaken bough, I do bestow as a gift, laden with acorns and with mast enough!"

Mast is food such as nuts; in this case, the acorns.

"Peace, man, for shame!" Pan said. "Quiet! We shall have both lambs and dames and flocks and herds and all, and all my pipes to make the glee and mirth; we don't meet now to brawl and quarrel."

Pipes are wind instruments that can be made from wood or reed.

"There's no problem, Pan," Faunus said. "We are all friends assembled hither to bid Queen Juno and her companions most humbly welcome hither. The presence of Diana, mistress of our woods and goddess of the hunt, will not be lacking. Her courtesy to all her friends, we know, is not at all scanty. Her consideration for her friends is abundant."

— 1.2 —

Pomona, goddess of orchards, arrived with her gift of fruit.

She said, "So, Pan, you have traveled no farther than this, and yet you had a head start on me? Why, then, Pomona with her fruit comes in good time enough, I see.

"Come on a while; like friends, we venture forth with the bounty of the country.

"Do you think, Faunus, that these goddesses will accept our gifts kindly and value them?"

"Yes, doubtless," Faunus answered, "for I shall tell thee, dame, it is better to give a thing, a token of love, to a mighty person or a king than to a rude and barbarous peasant who is bad and basely born, for the gentleman gently takes a token of love that often the peasant will scorn."

"You say the truth," Pan said. "I may say that to thee because I myself have given good plump lambs to Mercury, to Phoebus Apollo, and to Jove. And to a country lass, indeed, I have offered all their dams — ewes — and played my pipe and prayed to no avail to get the lass, and fruitlessly I have ranged about the grove."

Pomona said, "God Pan, your kissing in corners is what makes your flock so thin, and makes you look so lean."

"Well said, wench," Pan said affectionately, "but you mean some other thing."

The "some other thing" is more advanced than kissing.

"Yeah, jest it out until it go alone," Pomona said.

"Go it alone" indicates independent action. Pomona may have meant 1) "... jest it out until you are the only one laughing," or 2) "... jest it out until you begin having sex with yourself by masturbating."

"But marvel where we miss fair Flora all this merry morn," Pomona added. "Make jokes all you like, but where is Flora?"

"I have some news," Faunus said. "Look, and you can see where she is. She is coming."

— 1.3 —

Flora entered the scene.

Pan said, "Flora, well met, and for the pains you have taken, we poor country gods remain thy debtors. We are obliged to you."

As goddess of flowers and gardens, Flora made beautiful things grow. She had decorated this area with flowers in preparation for the arrival of the goddesses.

Flora said, "Believe me, Pan, not all thy lambs and ewes, nor, Faunus, all thy vigorous bucks and does — but that I have been taught well to know what duty I owe to the hills and valleys — could have persuaded me to do so strange a toil as to enrich this fine, brilliant soil with so many flowers."

"But tell me, wench," Faunus asked, "have you done it so neatly, indeed, in order that heaven itself may wonder at the deed?"

"Iris, goddess of the rainbow, in her splendor and finery, does not adorn her arch with such variety," Flora said. "Nor does the Milky-white Way in the frosty night sky appear as fair and beautiful in sight as do now these fields and groves and sweetest bowers, strewn and adorned with multi-colored flowers, along the bubbling brooks and silver stream that in their beds do in silence slide."

Flora then made a reference to Phoebe, which is another name for Diana, goddess of the hunt and of woods.

"The water-flowers and lilies on the banks, like blazing comets, all bloom in ranks. Under the hawthorn and the poplar tree, where sacred Phoebe may delight to be, the primrose, and the purple hyacinth, the dainty violet, and the wholesome mint plant, the double daisy, and the cowslip, queen of summer flowers, overlook the green grassy area.

"And round about the valley as you pass, you may not see the grass because of the many peeping flowers.

"I, the Queen of Flowers, have prepared a second spring so that the mighty Juno, and the rest, may well and boldly think themselves to be welcome guests on the hills of Ida — my flowers will show that they are welcome."

Silvanus asked, "Thou gentle nymph, what thanks shall we repay to thee who have made our fields and woods so gay?"

Instead of answering the question, Flora described the gifts that she had brought the goddesses: She had made their portraits out of flowers.

Flora said, "Silvanus, when it is thy good fortune to see my workmanship in portraying all the three goddesses, you will marvel.

"First I portrayed stately Juno with her elegant bearing and grace, her robes, her fine linen clothing, her small crown, and her scepter of office. This picture made of yellow oxlips bright as burnished gold would make thee marvel."

Pomona said, "It is a rare device, and Flora, by God, has well painted Juno yellow because of her jealousy."

Juno was very jealous of her husband, Jupiter, king of the gods, because of his many affairs with immortal goddesses and mortal women.

Flora said, "I have made Pallas' portrait in flowers of red hue and colors. Her plumes of feathers decorating her helmet, her lance, the

Gorgon's head, her trailing tresses of long hair that hang flaring round, of July-flowers so planted in the ground, in such a way that, trust me, sirs, whoever did see the cunning, skillful work would at a blush suppose it to be she."

Pallas is Pallas Athena, goddess of wisdom; she is a notable warrior. Her shield depicted the head of the Gorgon Medusa, who had snakes for hair.

"Good Flora, I swear by my flock," Pan said, "that it was very good to dress her entirely in red that resembles blood."

Flora said, "I made the portrait of fair Venus of sweet violets in blue, with other flowers inserted for changes of hue. Her plumes, her pendants, bracelets, and her rings, her dainty fan, and twenty other things, her gay cloak waving in the wind, and every part in color and in suitable kind. And as for her wreath of roses, she would not dare to compare it with Flora's cunning counterfeit portrait.

"So that whatever living person shall chance to see these goddesses, each placed as befits her social status, portrayed by Flora's workmanship alone, must say that art and nature have met in one."

Silvanus said, "A dainty portrait that lays Venus down in blue, the color that commonly betokens loyalty."

He was being ironic because Venus, the goddess of beauty and sexual passion, was not associated with loyalty. She had had a famous affair with Mars, god of war. She also had affairs with other gods and with mortals.

Flora said, "I have prepared this piece of work, composed of many a flower, and well laid in at the entrance of the bower where Phoebe — Diana — means to make this royal meeting."

"Have they yet descended from the heavens, Flora?" Pomona said. "Tell us, so that if they have we may go to meet them on the way."

"That shall not be necessary," Flora said. "They are near at hand by this time, and the head of their procession is a nymph named Rhanis.

"Juno left her chariot long ago, and she has returned her peacocks by her rainbow. Splendidly, as becomes the wife of Jove, she honors our grove with her presence."

Peacocks pulled Juno's chariot. After Juno got out of the chariot, the peacocks used the rainbow as a road to take her chariot back to the top of Mount Olympus, home of the major gods and goddesses.

Flora continued, "Fair Venus has let her sparrows fly, to tend on her and make her melody. Her turtledoves and her swans are unyoked and flicker near her side for company."

Venus sometimes traveled in a chariot drawn by swans and turtledoves. Swallows were sacred to her.

Flora continued, "Pallas has set her tigers loose to feed, commanding them to wait until she has need of them."

Pallas' chariot was usually pulled by horses, but on this occasion it may have been pulled by tigers.

Flora continued, "Hitherward with proud and stately pace, to do us honor in the sylvan hunting ground, Juno the wife and sister of King Jove, the warlike Pallas, and the Queen of Love march, similar to the pomp of heaven above."

Pan said, "Pipe, Pan, for joy, and let thy shepherds sing. Never shall any age forget this memorable thing."

Flora said, "Clio, the sagest of the Nine Sisters, to do observance to this divine dame, lady of learning and of chivalry, has here arrived in fair assembly, and wandering up and down the untrodden paths, sings sweet songs of praise of Pallas through the wood."

The Nine Sisters are the Muses; Clio is the Muse of History.

Pomona said, "Listen, Flora, Faunus! Here is melody — a chorus of birds that is more than ordinary."

Birds sang.

Pan said, "The innocent birds make mirth; we would do them wrong, Pomona, if we would not bestow an echo to their song."

All the gods and goddesses who were in sight sang about Mount Ida:

"*O Ida, O Ida, O Ida, happy hill!*

"*This honor done to Ida may it continue still [always]!*"

The Muses, who were out of sight, sang:

"*Ye country gods that in this Ida won [live],*

"*Bring down your gifts of welcome,*

"*For honor done to Ida.*"

The gods and goddesses who were in sight sang about Mount Ida:

"*Behold, in sign of joy we sing.*

"*And signs of joyful welcome bring.*

"*For honor done to Ida.*"

The Muses, who were out of sight, sang:

"*The Muses give you melody to gratulate this chance,*

"*And Phoebe, chief of sylvan chace, commands you all to dance.*"

The phrase "to gratulate this chance" meant "to joyfully welcome this opportunity."

The phrase "chief of sylvan chace" meant "goddess of the woodland hunting area."

The gods and goddesses who were in sight sang:

"*Then round in a circle our sportance [sportive activity] must be,*

"*Hold hands in a hornpipe, all gallant in glee.*"

Everybody danced to a tune performed on a hornpipe.

The Muses, who were out of sight, sang:

"*Reverence, reverence, most humble reverence!*"

The gods and goddesses who were in sight sang:

"*Most humble reverence!*"

— 1.4 —

Juno, Pallas, and Venus entered the scene, with the nymph Rhanis leading the way.

Pan sang solo:

"*The God of Shepherds, and his mates,*

*"With country cheer salutes your states,*
*"Fair, wise, and worthy as you be.*
*"And thank the gracious ladies three*
*"For honor done to Ida."*

Juno said, "Venus, what shall I say? For, although I am a divine dame, this welcome and this melody exceed these wits of mine."

Venus replied, "Believe me, Juno, as I am called the Sovereign of Love, these rare delights in pleasures surpass the banquets of King Jove."

Pallas said, "Then, Venus, I conclude that it easily may be seen that in her chaste and pleasant walks fair Phoebe is a queen."

Phoebe, aka Diana, is a chaste and virgin goddess, as is Pallas.

Rhanis said, "Divine Pallas, and you sacred dames, Juno and Venus, honored by your names, Juno, the wife and sister of King Jove, and Fair Venus, the lady-president and presiding goddess of love, if any entertainment in this place that can provide only what is homely, rude, and rustic does please your godheads and divine natures to accept graciously, that gracious thought shall be our happiness.

"My mistress Diana, this right well I know, for love that to this presence she does owe, accounts more honor done to her this day, than ever before in these woods of Ida.

"And as for our country gods, I dare be bold to say that they make such cheer, your presence to behold, such jouisance — such mirth, and such merriment — as nothing else could make their mind more content.

"And that you do believe it to be so, fair goddesses, your lovely looks do show. In short, it remains, in order to confirm what I have said, that you deign to pass along to Diana's walk, where among her troop of maidens she awaits the fair arrival of her welcome friends."

"And we will wait with all observance due," Flora said, "and do just honor to this heavenly crew."

"Juno, before thou go, I — the God of Shepherds — intend to bestow a lamb on thee," Pan said.

"I, Faunus, high gamekeeper in Diana's hunting grounds, present a fawn to Lady Venus' grace," Faunus said.

"I, Silvanus, give to Pallas' deity this gallant bough torn from the oak tree," Silvanus said.

"To them who do this honor to our fields, poor Pomona gives her mellow apples," Pomona said.

"And, gentle gods," Juno said, "these signs of your goodwill we accept graciously, and we shall always accept them graciously."

Venus said, "And, Flora, I say this to thee among the rest — thy workmanship comparing with the best, let it suffice thy cunning and learning to have the power to call King Jove from out of his heavenly bower. If thou had a lover, Flora, believe me, I think thou would bedeck him gallantly.

"But we must go on: Lead the way, Rhanis, you who know the painted — decorated with flowers — paths of pleasant Ida."

— 1.5 —

Paris and Oenone talked together. Paris was a prince of Troy, and Oenone was a nymph whom he was courting.

Paris said, "Oenone, while we are here until we are disposed to walk, tell me what shall be the subject of our talk? Thou have a number of pretty tales in your head — I dare say that no nymph in the woods of Ida has more: Again, in addition to thy sweet alluring face, in telling your tales thou have a special grace. So then, please, sweetheart, tell some pretty thing — some pleasing trifle that from thy pleasant wit does spring."

"Paris, my heart's contentment and my choice, play thou thy pipe, and I will use my voice," Oenone said, "and so thy just request shall not be denied, and it will be time well spent, and both of us will be satisfied."

"Well, gentle nymph, although thou do me wrong, me who cannot tune my pipe to play accompaniment to a song, I choose this once to accompany you, Oenone, for thy sake, and so I will undertake this leisure-time task."

They sat under a tree together.

"And on which subject, then, shall be my roundelay — my song?" Oenone said. "For thou have heard my store of stories long before now, I dare say:

"How Saturn divided his kingdom long ago to Jove, to Neptune, and to Dis below."

Saturn actually had to be forced to give up his kingdom. Saturn was the father of Jupiter, Neptune, and Dis. His sons rebelled against him, overthrew him, and divided the earth among themselves. Jupiter became the god of the sky, Neptune became the god of the sea, and Dis, aka Pluto, became the god of the Land of the Dead. As the king of the gods, Jupiter exerted the most power over the land.

Oenone continued:

"How mighty men made foul and unsuccessful war against the gods and the state of Jupiter."

A race of Giants, including Otis and Ephialtes, fought the Olympian gods for supremacy, but the Olympians defeated the Giants.

Oenone continued:

"How Phorcys' imp, who was so trim and fair, who tangled Neptune in her golden hair, became a Gorgon because of her lewd misdeed."

Phorcys was a sea god whose children included Medusa, whom Oenone called an imp. Medusa had an affair with Neptune in a temple dedicated to Pallas, and Pallas punished her by turning her hair into snakes and making her face so horrible that any mortal who looked at it turned to stone.

Oenone added, "This is a pretty fable, Paris, for you to read. It is a piece of cunning, trust me, and it makes this point: That wealth and beauty alter men to stones."

Medusa had wealth and beauty, but she became a monster that turned men who saw her to stone. In other cases, a woman of wealth and beauty can also ruin a man.

Readers who know about the Trojan War may be thinking of Helen of Troy right now.

Oenone continued:

"How Salmacis, resembling idleness, turns men to women all through wantonness and lewd behavior."

Salmacis was a nymph who fell in love with Aphroditus, son of Venus and Mercury. He rejected her advances, but she hugged him close to her and prayed never to be separated from him. Their two bodies grew together, and they became Hermaphroditus, the god of hermaphroditism and intersexuality. Hermaphroditus then cursed a fountain to make it turn men to women; the fountain was named after Salmacis.

Oenone continued:

"How Pluto caught Queen Ceres' daughter thence, and what did follow of that love-offence."

Proserpine, whose Greek name was Persephone, was picking flowers when Pluto, god of the Land of the Dead, kidnapped her, took her to the Underworld, and made her Queen of the Land of the Dead. Ceres, the goddess of agriculture whose Greek name was Demeter, mourned, and because she mourned, nothing would grow. Jupiter arranged an agreement with Pluto that allowed Proserpine to spend six months of every year in the Land of the Living and the other six months in the Land of the Dead. When Proserpine is in the Land of the Dead, winter occurs.

Oenone continued:

"Of Daphne turned into the laurel-tree, a tale that shows a mirror — a good example — of virginity."

The god Apollo fell in love with the nymph Daphne, who ran from him, who pursued her. She prayed to her father, a river-god, for help, and he transformed her into a laurel tree.

Oenone continued:

"How fair Narcissus staring at his own image, rebukes scorn, and tells how beauty does vanish."

Narcissus was a beautiful man who scorned the love of both Echo (a nymph) and Ameinias (a young man). Before committing suicide, Ameinias prayed to Nemesis, goddess of retribution, to punish Narcissus. She made him fall in love with his own reflection in a stream. He continually loved and looked at it as he wasted away.

Oenone continued:

"How cunning Philomela's needle tells what force in love and what intelligence in sorrow dwell."

Philomela was an Athenian princess who was raped by her sister's husband, Tereus, who cut out her tongue so that she could not tell anyone that he had raped her. Philomela wove a tapestry, however, that revealed the rape and rapist.

Oenone continued:

"What pains unhappy souls endure in hell, they say because on earth they lived not well — Ixion's wheel, proud Tantalus' pining woe, Prometheus' torment, and many more."

Ixion, who violated proper guest-host relations, was bound to a continually spinning fiery wheel in the Land of the Dead. Among his sins was attempting to seduce Juno while he was one of Jupiter's guests.

Tantalus, the father of Pelops, killed him, cooked him, and served him to the gods as a test of their intelligence. One goddess, Ceres, ate some of Pelops' shoulder before the trickery was discovered, and so he was outfitted with a shoulder made of ivory. The gods brought Pelops back to life and sentenced his father, Tantalus, to everlasting punishment in the Land of the Dead. He stands in a stream of water with fruit-bearing branches above his head. Whenever he stoops to drink, the water level lowers and the stream dries up. Whenever he reaches for fruit to eat, the wind blows the branches just out of his reach. He is forever thirsty and hungry, and water and fruit are always just out of his possession.

Prometheus, who was a Titan (one of the primordial — which means existing from the beginning of time — beings who ruled the Earth until Jupiter conquered them), stole fire from the gods and gave it to early Humankind. Jupiter punished Prometheus by chaining him to a rock and sending an eagle to devour his liver, which grew back each night so the eagle could devour it again the following day.

Oenone continued:

"How Danaus' daughters ply their endless task."

The fifty sons of Aegyptus wanted to marry the fifty daughters of Danaus. Danaus was suspicious of Aegyptus and his fifty sons, so he fled with his fifty daughters, but Aegyptus and his fifty sons pursued them. To avoid a battle, Danaus told his fifty daughters to marry the fifty sons of Aegyptus, but although he allowed the marriages to be performed he also ordered his fifty daughters to kill the fifty sons of Aegyptus. All of his daughters except Hypermnestra, who had married Lynceus, obeyed. Hypermnestra spared Lynceus because he treated her with respect and did not force her to have sex with him their first night together. The gods did not like what the forty-nine women who had killed their husbands had done, and so those forty-nine daughters are punished in the Land of the Dead with meaningless work. They are condemned to spend all their time trying to fill up with water a container that has a big leak and so can never be filled. Only one daughter avoided this eternal punishment.

Oenone continued:

"What toil the toil of Sisyphus does ask."

When Sisyphus was on his deathbed, he ordered his wife not to give his corpse a funeral. After his death, his spirit went to the Land of the Dead and complained to Pluto, King of the Dead, that he had not yet had a funeral. Pluto allowed him to return to the Land of the Living so that he could tell his wife to give him a funeral, but once he was back in the Land of the Living, he refused to return to the Land of the Dead. He lived to an advanced old age and then died again. Now he is forced to forever roll a boulder up a hill. Just as he reaches the top of the hill, he loses control of the boulder and it rolls back to the bottom of the hill again. Sisyphus can never accomplish this task, which has no value, and so his punishment is endless meaningless work.

Oenone continued:

"I know that all these tales are old and well known, yet, if thou will hear any tales, choose some of these because if you don't, believe me, Oenone has not many tales."

Paris said, "No, you choose whichever one you want, but since my skill does not compare with yours, start with a simple song that I can play upon this pipe of mine."

Oenone said, "There is a pretty sonnet, then, that we call 'Cupid's Curse': 'They who do change old love for new, please, gods, make it so that they change for worse!'

"The tune is fine and also quick; the message of the song will agree, Paris, with that same vow you made to me upon our poplar tree."

Paris had carved into a poplar tree his vow that he would always love Oenone.

"No better thing," Paris said. "Begin it, then. Oenone, thou shall see our music present the love that grows between thee and me."

They sang the song, and whenever Oenone sang solo, Paris played his pipe.

Oenone sang:

*"Fair and fair, and twice so fair,*
*"As fair as any may be;*

"*The fairest shepherd on our green,*
"*A love for any lady.*"
Paris sang:
"*Fair and fair, and twice so fair,*
"*As fair as any may be;*
"*Thy love is fair for thee alone,*
"*And for no other lady.*"
Oenone sang:
"*My love is fair, my love is gay,*
"*As fresh as bin [are] the flowers in May,*
"*And of my love my roundelay,*
"*My merry merry roundelay,*
"*Concludes with Cupid's curse —*
"*They that [who] do change old love for new.*
"*Pray gods they change for worse!*"
Paris and Oenone sang together:
"*They that [who] do change old love for new.*
"*Pray gods they change for worse!*"
Oenone sang:
"*Fair and fair, and twice so fair,*
"*As fair as any may be.*"
Paris sang:
"*Fair and fair, and twice so fair,*
"*As fair as any may be;*
"*Thy love is fair for thee alone,*
"*And for no other lady.*"
Oenone sang:
"*My love can pipe, my love can sing.*
"*My love can many a pretty thing,*
"*And of his lovely praises ring*
"*My merry merry roundelays,*
"*Amen to Cupid's curse,*

*"They that [who] do change old love for new.*
*"Pray gods they change for worse!"*
Paris sang:
*"They that [who] do change old love for new.*
*"Pray gods they change for worse!"*
Paris and Oenone sang together:
*"Fair and fair, and twice so fair,*
*"As fair as any may be."*
Now that the song was over, they stood up.

Oenone said, "Sweet shepherd, for Oenone's sake learn from this song, and keep thy love, and love thy choice, or else thou do her wrong."

The song was a warning: Those who reject an old love for a new love can change a good love for a worse love. Paris had chosen Oenone for his love; if he were to reject her and choose another love, then bad things could happen to him.

Paris said, "My vow is made and witnessed, the poplar tree will not start and tremble, nor shall my love for the nymph Oenone leave my breathing heart."

If Paris had made a false vow to love Oenone, then the poplar tree upon which Paris had carved his vow would start and tremble.

Paris continued, "I will go accompany thee on thy way, my flock are here behind, and I will have a lover's fee; they say that those who are unkissed are unkind."

The lover's fee is a kiss.

They exited.

# CHAPTER 2

— 2.1 —

Juno, Pallas, and Venus talked together.

Venus said, "But please, tell me, Juno, was what Pallas told me here about the tale of Echo true?"

Echo was a nymph who kept Juno distracted while her husband, Jupiter, conducted affairs with other nymphs. When Juno discovered what Echo was doing, Juno punished her by making her unable to form words on her own; instead, Echo could only repeat the last words that others had said.

Juno replied, "Echo was a nymph indeed, as Pallas told you. She was a walker, such as in these thickets dwells."

The word "walker" meant 1) walker in the forest, and 2) prostitute, as in "streetwalker."

Juno continued, "And as Pallas told what cunning and deceitful tricks Echo played with Juno, so she told the 'thanks' Echo got: She was a tattling trull — prostitute — to come at every call, and now, truly, she has neither tongue nor life at all."

According to Juno, Echo was a talkative whore who came at every call, but now she has neither voice nor life. Now Echo can only repeat the last words that others say. Because of that, she was unable to tell Narcissus effectively that she loved him, and so she had been forced to watch him as he died while staring at his reflection, unable to move away from it and eat and drink. After he died, she wasted away with mourning until all that was left was her voice.

Juno continued, "And though perhaps she was a help to Jove, and held me back with chat while he might court his love of the time, believe me, dames, I am of this opinion: He took but little pleasure in the minion. And whatsoever his escapades have been besides, I dare say for him that he never strayed so wide: A lovely nut-brown lass or lusty whore has the power perhaps to make a god a bull."

Jupiter enthusiastically engaged in affairs, but Juno, his wife, blamed the females he slept with for enticing him into having affairs. In one of his affairs, Jupiter fell in lust with the Phoenician woman Europa; he then assumed the form of a bull and carried her away to Crete. He had sex with her, and she gave birth to a boy who became King Minos of Crete.

"Much thanks, gentle Juno, for that jest," Venus said. "In faith, that item was worth all the rest."

The jest was that Jupiter did not enjoy his affairs. No one who knew Jupiter — other than Juno — would believe that.

"No matter, Venus, howsoever you scorn, my father Jove at that time wore the horn," Pallas said.

When he transformed into a bull, Jupiter wore horns on his head. Pallas was also alluding to the joke that cuckolds — men with unfaithful wives — wore invisible horns on their heads, and so she was suggesting that Juno had been unfaithful to Jupiter.

Juno tended to get revenge on the women her husband slept with instead of getting revenge on her husband by being unfaithful. But there is one story in which she gave birth to a child without Jupiter being the father. She did that to get revenge for Jupiter's giving birth to a goddess.

Pallas had been born — fully armed — when Jupiter suffered a tremendous headache that was so bad that he had another god split his head open. (According to myths, which often vary, either Pallas had no mother or Zeus had swallowed a pregnant goddess.) Pallas sprang out from the wound.

To get back at Zeus for giving birth to a goddess, Juno gave birth to Vulcan, the blacksmith god. Zeus was not the father. Supposedly, Juno impregnated herself, although Venus and Pallas are likely to believe that as much as they believe that Jupiter does not enjoy having affairs.

Juno said, "Had every wanton god above not had better luck, Venus, then heaven would be a pleasant park, and Mars a lusty buck."

In other words, the gods can easily enough find humans to seduce; if they could not, they would regard the abode of the gods as a happy hunting ground for lovers, and many goddesses would be having affairs with Mars, god of war.

Juno was alluding to the affair that Venus had had with Mars: The two had fallen in lust although Venus, the goddess of sexual passion, was married to Vulcan, the gifted blacksmith god. Vulcan learned of the affair, so he set a trap for the illicit lovers. He created fine chains that bound tightly, he placed the chains above his bed, and then he pretended to leave his mansion to journey abroad. Mars ran to Aphrodite and invited her to join him in Vulcan's bed, and together they ran to bed. Mars and Venus lay down in bed together, and then the chain snared them, locked together in lust.

Venus said, "Tut, Mars has horns to butt with, although no bull he shows; he never needs to mask in nets, and he fears no jealous woman's frowns."

Mars may have affairs, but the females he sleeps with, such as Venus, also have affairs, and so in a way he has the horns of a cuckold, although he never married. But Mars need not turn himself into a bull or wear masks or disguises that can be as easily seen through as nets — Jupiter's disguises seem to work only for a while, as Juno quickly becomes aware of them.

Juno replied, "Truly, the better it would be for Mars if he did turn himself into a bull as a disguise, for if he speaks too loudly, he must find some means to shadow and hide him: a net or else a cloud."

Of course, hiding under a net is a bad way for Mars to hide himself, but Juno was again alluding to Venus' being trapped in a net with Mars while engaged in the act of sex.

After Vulcan had captured the pair, he invited the gods and goddesses to come and laugh at them. The gods came and laughed, but the goddesses were embarrassed and stayed away.

"No more of this, fair goddesses," Pallas said. "Don't put on display your shames, as if you were standing all naked on display to the world, you who are such heavenly dames."

"Nay, Pallas," Juno said. "That's a common trick with Venus, well we know, and all the gods in heaven have seen her naked long ago."

The gods had seen Venus naked when she was trapped with Mars in Vulcan's net.

Venus replied, "And then she — me, Venus — was so fair and bright, and lovely and so fine, as Mars is to Venus' liking, and she will take her pleasure with him. And — but I don't wish here to make a comparison of Mars with Jove — Mars is no ranger, Juno, but Jupiter can be found in every open grove."

A ranger is a 1) gamekeeper, or 2) chaser after females.

"We have had too much of this wrangling," Pallas said. "We wander far, and the skies begin to scowl. Let's retire to Diana's bower, for the weather will be foul."

A storm of thunder and lightning passed overhead. Até arrived and rolled the golden ball toward the three goddesses, crying *"Fatum Trojae — the Fate of Troy!"*

Juno picked up the golden ball and said, "Pallas, the storm is past and gone, and Phoebus Apollo clears the skies, and — look! — behold a ball of gold, a fair and worthy prize!"

Venus examined the ball closely. It had writing on it: a posey, or short inscription.

She said, "This posey says that the apple is to be given to the fairest. So then it is mine, for Venus is called the fairest of we three goddesses."

The fairest goddess is the most beautiful goddess. Beauty, however, can appear in many forms. It need not only be physical beauty.

"The fairest here, since fair is meant, am I," Pallas said. "You do me wrong. And if the fairest must have it, to me it does belong."

"Then Juno may not enjoy it, so every one says," Juno said. "But I will prove myself the fairest, before I lose it."

They read the posey.

Juno said, "The brief is this — '*Detur pulcherrimae*, let this to the fairest given be, to the fairest of the three' — and I am she."

"*Detur pulcherrimae*" is Latin for "Let it be given to the most beautiful."

Pallas said, "'*Detur pulcherrimae*, let this to the fairest given be, to the fairest of the three' — and I am she."

Venus said, "'*Detur pulcherrimae*, let this to the fairest given be, to the fairest of the three' — and I am she."

"My face is fair," Juno said, "but yet the majesty that all the gods in heaven have seen in me has made them choose me of the seven planets to be the wife of Jove and queen of heaven.

"If, then, this prize is to be only bequeathed to beauty, I am the only she who wins this prize."

The seven planets known to the Elizabethans include five that were named after gods: Mercury, Venus, Mars, Jupiter, and Saturn; the Elizabethans also considered the Moon and Sun to be planets.

Juno considered the fairest to be the goddess with the most majesty. None of the seven planets was named after her, but she considered herself to be a luminary worthy of being wed to the king of the gods. Juno, however, was associated with the Moon.

Venus said, "This proves that Venus is the fairest: Venus is the lovely Queen of Love: The name of Venus is indeed but beauty, and men call me the fairest above all — the fairest *par excellence*.

"If, then, this prize is to be only bequeathed to beauty, I am the only she who wins this prize."

Venus considered the fairest to be the goddess with the greatest physical beauty.

Pallas, the goddess of wisdom, said, "To insist on the definition of beauty as you define it, believe me, ladies, is but to mistake it. The beauty that this ingenious prize must win is not outward beauty, but beauty that dwells within. Examine it as and however you please, and you shall find, this beauty is the beauty of the mind.

"This fairness is in general called virtue, which has many distinct parts. This beauty is called wisdom, the goddess of which I am worthily appointed by heaven. And look how much the mind, the better part, does surpass the body in merit — by so much the mistress of those divine gifts excels thy beauty and that state of thine.

"If, then, this prize is to be only bequeathed to beauty, I am the only she who wins this prize."

Pallas considered the fairest to be the goddess with the most wisdom.

Venus said, "No, Pallas, with your permission let me say that you are completely on the wrong track. We must not define 'beauty' as you have, but instead take the sense as it is plainly meant. I am content to let the fairest have it."

"Our arguments will be infinite, I trust, unless we agree on some other way of awarding the golden ball," Pallas said. "Here's none, I think, disposed to yield, and none but will with words maintain the field and defend our ground."

"So then, if you agree, to avoid a tedious grudge, let us refer the question of who gets the golden ball to the sentence of a judge," Juno said. "Whoever comes next to this place, let him bestow the ball and end the case."

"If we do that, it cannot go wrong with me at all," Venus said.

"I am agreed, however it befall," Pallas said. "And yet by common opinion, so may it be, I may be said to be the fairest of the three."

Seeing Paris coming toward them, Juno said, "Look yonder — that shepherd swain is he who must be umpire in this controversy!"

Each goddess was confident that an impartial judge would choose her as the fairest and award her the golden ball.

— **2.2** —

Paris entered the scene. Although he was a prince of Troy, he was raised as a shepherd. Because a prophecy had stated that he would be the downfall of Troy, he was exposed as an infant on the slopes of Mount Ida. A she-bear suckled him, and then a herdsman sheltered him and raised him as a shepherd. Perhaps he knew now that he was a prince of Troy, but he spent much time on Mount Ida courting Oenone and working as a shepherd.

Venus said, "Juno, in this happy time, I accept the man as our judge. It seems by his looks that he knows some skill of love."

Paris said to himself, "The nymph Oenone has gone, and I, all solitary and oppressed with melancholy, must make my way to tend my sheep. This day (or else my shepherd's skill fails me) will bring me surpassing good or surpassing ill. My shepherd's intuition says that either something very good or something very bad will happen to me today."

Juno said to Paris, "Shepherd, don't be astonished, although suddenly thus thou have arrived accidentally among us three, who are not earthly but are divine goddesses. Our names are Juno, Pallas, and Venus.

"Nor should you fear to speak because of reverence of the place. You have been chosen to judge and end a hard and unsettled case. This golden apple, look — don't ask from where it came — is to be given to the fairest dame!

"And the fairest is, neither she, nor she" — Juno surreptitiously indicated Venus and Pallas — "but she whom, shepherd, thou shall name to be the fairest. This is thy charge; fulfill it without offence, and she who wins shall give thee recompense."

"Fulfill it without offence" is ambiguous. It can mean 1) "fulfill it without causing offense," or 2) "fulfill it and your judgment will not cause offense."

Because all three goddesses wanted to be awarded the prize, it is hard to see how Paris could award the golden ball to one goddess without offending the other two goddesses.

Pallas said, "Don't be afraid to speak, for we have chosen thee, since in this case we cannot be the judges."

Venus said, "And, shepherd, say that I am the fairest, and thou shall win a good reward for doing so."

Juno said, "Nay, shepherd, look upon my stately grace, because the pomp that belongs to Juno's mace — symbol of authority — thou may not see; and think Queen Juno's name, to whom old shepherds give the credit for works of fame, is mighty, and may easily suffice to gain a golden prize at Phoebus' hand."

Juno wanted to be awarded the golden ball because of her majestic bearing. The gods, however, cannot reveal their full majesty to human beings, as shown in this story: Jupiter had an affair with the mortal woman Semele, to whom he had made an inviolable oath to grant her what she wished. After he had sex with her, Semele said that she wanted to see him in his full glory. Because his oath was inviolable, he granted her wish, but the sight of Jupiter in his full glory incinerated her.

Phoebus Apollo was the god who drove the Sun-chariot across the sky. Because the goddesses found the golden ball only after a storm passed and the Sun came out, they may have thought that the golden ball metaphorically came from Phoebus Apollo's hand.

Juno continued, "And for thy reward, since I am queen of riches, shepherd, I will reward thee with great monarchies, empires, and kingdoms, heaps of solid gold, elaborately made scepters and diadems, rich robes of sumptuous workmanship and cost, and a thousand things whereof I make no boast. The earth upon which thou tread shall be of the Tagus River's sands that are mixed with gold, and the Xanthus River shall run liquid gold for thee to wash thy hands. And if thou prefer to tend thy flock, and not from them to flee, their fleeces shall be curled gold to please their master's eye. And last, to set thy heart on fire, give this one fruit to me, and, shepherd, look, this tree of gold will I bestow on thee!"

Using divine magic, Juno created a show for Paris: A tree of gold, laden with diadems and crowns of gold, rose from out of the earth.

Juno said, "The ground whereupon it grows, the grass, the root are of gold, the body and the bark are of gold, all glistening to behold, the leaves are of burnished gold, the fruits that thereon grow are diadems set with pearl in gold, in gorgeous glistening show. And if this tree of gold in compensation may not suffice, then demand a grove of golden trees, as long as Juno carries away the prize."

The golden tree sank into the earth.

Juno was offering Paris the rule of cities and great wealth.

Pallas said to Paris, "I choose not to tempt thee with decaying wealth, which is debased by lack of vigorous health."

Excess wealth can cause dissipation, which leads to ill health.

Pallas continued, "But if thou have a mind to fly above and achieve loftier ambitions, crowned with fame, near the seat of Jove, if thou aspire to wisdom's worthiness, of which thou may not see the brightness" — this was true; Paris was not a wise man — "if thou desire honor of chivalry, to be renowned for happy victory, to fight it out, and in the open battlefield to shroud thee under Pallas' warlike shield, to prance on armored steeds, this honor I myself as a reward shall bestow on thee! And as encouragement for you to award the golden ball to me, thou may see what famous knights Dame Pallas' warriors are — look! In Pallas' honor here they come, marching along with the sound of thundering drums."

Using divine magic, Pallas created a show for Paris: Nine armored knights treaded a warlike march to the music of drum and fife, and then they marched away again.

The Nine Knights were probably the Nine Worthies. All of them were warriors. Three were pagans: Hector of Troy, Alexander the Great, and Julius Caesar. Three were Jews: Joshua, King David, and Judas

Maccabeus. Three were Christians: King Arthur, Charlemagne, and Godfrey of Boullion, who was famous for being a leader in the First Crusade.

Some of them were from the future, but Paris would have recognized Hector of Troy: Hector was his brother.

Pallas was offering Paris mightiness as a warrior.

Venus said, "Come, shepherd, come, sweet shepherd, look at me. These alarums — calls to arms — are too hot and dangerous for thee: But if thou will give me the golden ball, Cupid my boy shall have it to play with, with the result that, whenever this apple he shall see, the god of love himself shall think on thee. And he will tell thee to look and choose, and he will wound wherever thy fancy's object shall be found. And merrily when he shoots, he does not miss."

If Paris awards the golden ball to Venus, then her son Cupid, the god of love, will make any woman Paris desires fall in love with him.

Venus continued, "And I will give thee many a lovely and loving kiss and come and play with thee on Ida here, and if thou will love a face that has no peer, a gallant girl, a lusty paramour, who can give thee thy bellyful of sexual entertainment and will make all thy veins beat with joy, here is a lass of Venus' court, my boy. Here, gentle shepherd, here's for thee a piece, the fairest face, the flower of gallant Greece."

Using divine magic, Venus created a show for Paris:

Helen, splendidly dressed, entered the scene with four cupids — cherubs — attending on her, each having his fan in his hand to fan fresh air in her face.

She then sang this song:

*"Se Diana nel cielo è una stella*

*"Chiara e lucente, piena di splendore,*

*"Che porge luc' all' affanato cuore;*

*"Se Diana nel ferno è una dea*

*"Che da conforto all' anime dannate,*

*"Che per amor son morte desperate;*

*"Se Dian, ch' in terra è delle ninfe*

*"Reina imperativa di dolei fiori,*

*"Tra bosch' e selve da morte a pastori;*

*"Io son un Diana dolce e rara,*

*"Che con li guardi io posso far guerra*

*"A Dian' infern' in cielo, e in terra."*

Helen sang in Italian. Henry Morley (1822-1894) translated her song into English:

*"If Diana in Heaven is a star,*

*"Clear and shining, full of splendor,*

*"Who gives light to the troubled heart;*

*"If Diana in Hell is a goddess*

*"Who gives comfort to the condemned souls,*

*"That [Who] have died in despair through love;*

*"If Diana who is on earth is of the nymphs*

*"The empress queen of the sweet flowers,*

*"Among thickets and woods giving death to the shepherds;*

*"I am a Diana sweet and pure,*

*"Who with my glamour can give battle*

*"To Dian of Hell, in Heaven or on earth."*

Diana was considered a triple deity. In Heaven, she was Luna, goddess of the Moon. (Other goddesses, such as Juno, were also associated with the Moon.) In Hell, she was Hecate, goddess of witchcraft. On earth she was Diana, goddess of the hunt.

Helen, having sung her song that acknowledged that love can cause distress and death, exited.

Venus was offering Paris success in love — or at least success in lust.

Paris said, "Most heavenly dames, there was never a man like I, a poor shepherd swain, so fortunate and unfortunate. Even the least of these delights that you devise are able to enrapt and dazzle human eyes.

"But since my silence may not be pardoned and I must appoint which is the fairest she, then pardon me, most sacred dames, since only one, and not all, by Paris' judgment must have this golden ball.

"Thy beauty, stately Juno dame divine, that similar to Phoebus Apollo's golden beams does shine, approves itself to be most excellent."

Paris praised Juno's beauty despite not awarding the golden ball to her. He neglected to praise Pallas' beauty despite not awarding the golden ball to her.

Paris continued, "But that fair face that most delights me, since fair, fair dames, is neither she nor she" — he pointed to Juno and Pallas — "but she whom I shall judge to be fairest — that face is hers who is called the Queen of Love, whose sweetness does both gods and creatures move. And if the fairest face deserves the ball, fair Venus, ladies, bears it away from you all."

He gave the golden ball to Venus.

Venus said, "And in this ball does Venus more delight than in seeing her lovely boy fair Cupid. Come, shepherd, come. Sweet Venus is thy friend, no matter how thou offend other gods."

Venus and Paris exited.

Juno said, "But he shall rue and curse the dismal day in which his Venus carried the ball away, and heaven and earth shall be just witnesses that I will revenge it on his family."

Pallas said, "Well, Juno, whether we are willing or unwilling, Venus has taken the apple from us both."

# CHAPTER 3

— 3.1 —

Colin, a shepherd who was in love with a young woman named Thestylis, sang this love song:

"*Oh, gentle Love, ungentle [unkind] for thy deed,*

"*Thou mak'st [make] my heart*

"*A bloody mark*

"*With piercing shot to bleed!*"

Colin was complaining because Cupid, god of Love, had shot him with an arrow and made him fall in love.

Colin continued singing:

"*Shoot soft [gently and carefully], sweet Love, for fear thou shoot amiss [thou miss],*

"*For fear too keen [sharp]*

"*Thy arrows been,*

"*And hit the heart where my beloved is.*"

Colin wanted Cupid to shoot his (Colin's) beloved with an arrow so she would return his (Colin's) love.

Colin continued singing:

"*Too fair that fortune were, nor never I*

"*Shall be so blest,*

"*Among the rest,*

"*That Love shall seize on her by sympathy.*

"*Then since with Love my prayers bear no boot [have proven to be useless],*

"*This doth [does] remain*

"*To cease my pain, I take [receive] the wound, and die at Venus' foot.*"

Colin was complaining that he has not had the good fortune for Cupid to take pity on him and so he will just have to die of unrequited love.

Colin then exited.

Hobbinol, Diggon, and Thenot talked together. They were shepherd friends of Colin's.

Hobbinol said, "Poor Colin, woeful man, thy life predetermined by love, what strange fit, what malady, is this that thou do experience?"

Diggon said, "Either Love is completely void of medicine, or Love's our common ruin, which gives us poison to bring us low, and lets us lack medicine."

This Love is Venus, Queen of Love, who excited sexual passion in mortals and immortals.

Hobbinol said, "How odd that Love was ever reverenced by naive shepherd swains! Perhaps Love hurts them most who most might bear their pains."

Love can hurt people when it is not returned, but if one successfully pursues the loved one, then one's pains are often richly rewarded.

Using a nickname, Thenot said, "Hobbin, it is some other god who cherishes her sheep, for surely this Love does nothing else but make our herdsmen weep."

"Her sheep" are mortals: the shepherds. According to Thenot, Venus does not care about her "sheep" because she causes them pain by making them feel passion. Sometimes she did this by asking her son, Cupid, to shoot them with an arrow.

Diggon said, "And what an event is this, I say, when all our woods rejoice because of the visit of the three goddesses, for Colin thus to be denied his young and lovely choice: Thestylis?"

Thenot said, "Thestylis indeed is known to be so fresh and fair that well it is for thee that Colin and Nature have been thy friend and made it so that Cupid could not see you. If Cupid had seen you instead of Colin, he would have shot you with an arrow and made you love a woman who would not return your love."

Hobbinol asked, "And whither wends yonder Colin, the unsuccessful swain? He is like the stricken deer that seeks dictamnum for his wound within our forest here."

Dictamnum is an herb that deer eat to help heal their wounds, including wounds made with arrows.

Diggon said, "He wends his way to greet the Queen of Love, who is in these woods, with mirthless lays to make complaint to Venus about her son."

Colin was going to see Venus and sing sad songs complaining about the love — unrequited — that her son Cupid is making him feel.

Thenot said, "Ah, Colin, thou are entirely deceived! Venus dallies with her son, and closes her eyes to all his wanton pranks, and she thinks thy love is only a trifle."

Hobbinol said, "Then leave him to his luckless love and let him endure his fate. His sore is festering entirely too much, and our comfort comes too late."

Diggon said, "Although Thestylis is the scorpion that breaks his sweet assault, yet will Rhamnusia take vengeance on Thestylis' disdainful fault."

A scorpion is a catapult. In a military metaphor, Colin had tried to conquer Thestylis and win her love, but she had repulsed him. Because Diggon was Colin's friend, he (and the other shepherds) regarded Thestylis' rejection of Colin's love as wrong.

Thenot said, "Look, yonder comes the lovely nymph, who in these Ida vales plays with Amyntas' lusty boy — Paris — and caresses him in the dales!"

Vales and dales are valleys.

Hobbinol said, "Thenot, I think her mood has changed, her mirthful looks are laid to rest, she frolics not; I pray to god that the lad has not beguiled the maiden!"

He was hoping that Paris had not deceived Oenone with a false promise of love.

Oenone entered the scene. She was wearing a wreath of poplar on her head. Paris had carved into a poplar tree his vow that he would always love Oenone.

Oenone said to herself, "Beguiled, disdained, and out of love! Live long, thou poplar tree, and let thy letters of the vow Paris carved grow in length, to witness this with me. Ah, Venus, if not for my reverence of thy sacred name, I might account it blame for thee to steal a naive maiden's love! And if the tales I hear, and blush to repeat, are true, thou do me wrong to leave the plains and dally out of sight. False, disloyal Paris, this was not thy vow, when thou and I were one, to wander and exchange old love for new, but now those days are gone. But I will find and visit the goddess so that she may read thy vow, and I will fill these woods with my laments for thy unhappy deed."

Hobbinol said, "She has so fair a face, and yet so foul a thought harbors in Paris' breast! Thy hopes are ruined, poor nymph, and thy luck is worse than all the rest."

Seeing Paris' friends, Oenone said, "Ah, shepherds, you are full of wiles, and whet your wits on books, and enrapt poor maidens with music pipes and songs, and sweet alluring looks!"

Diggon said to her, "Don't wrongly criticize all shepherds because of Paris' misdeed. There are those who keep flocks who never chose any but one woman, and have never tricked a woman in love with false vows."

"False Paris is not one of those faithful shepherds," Oenone said. "His faithless double deed — vowing love to two women — will hurt many shepherds who otherwise might go near to success."

Thenot said, "Poor Colin, that is ill for thee, who are as true in trust to thy sweet smart — Thestylis, who causes you pain — as Paris has been unjust to his nymph."

"Ah, well is the woman whom Colin will win because he will have no other love!" Oenone said. "And woe is me, my luck is loss, my pains arouse no pity!"

Hobbinol said, "Farewell, fair nymph, since he who gave you the wound is the only man who must heal it. There grows on Dame Nature's ground no herb with such healing power."

The shepherds Hobbinol, Diggon, and Thenot exited.

— 3.4 —

Mercury, who wore winged sandals and a winged hat and carried a winged staff called a caduceus, and some of Vulcan's Cyclopes, one of whom was named Pyracmon, entered the scene.

Vulcan's Cyclopes were one-eyed giants who helped the god in his blacksmithing work. Mercury's job was to carry messages from Jupiter, king of the gods.

Seeing the nymph Oenone, Mercury said to one of the Cyclopes, "Here is a nymph who sadly sits, and she likely can tell us some news, Pyracmon, about the jolly swain we seek. I dare to wage my wings that the lass is in love because she looks so bleak and thin out of anger or out of grief, but I will begin to talk with her."

"Swain" can mean shepherd or lover. They were seeking Paris, who was both.

Oenone said to herself, "Break out, poor heart, and complain in song — moving even the mountain flocks — about what a proud repulse and thankless scorn thou have received from love."

Mercury said, "She sings; sirs, be hushed a while."

Oenone sang her lament as she sat:

"*Melpomene, the Muse of tragic songs,*

"*With mournful tunes, in stole [a robe] of dismal hue [color],*

"*Assist a silly [naïve] nymph to wail her woe,*

"*And leave thy lusty [vigorous] company behind.*"

Epic poets such as Homer and Virgil began their epic poems with invocations to a Muse or to all the Muses to assist them in creating their poems.

Oenone continued:

*"Thou luckless wreath! becomes not me [it is not fitting for me] to wear*
*"The poplar tree for triumph of my love:*
*"Then, as my joy, my pride of love, is left,*
*"Be thou unclothed of thy lovely green;"*

This means: Let your lovely green leaves fall, poplar wreath.

Oenone continued:

*"And in thy leaves my fortune written be,"*

This culture believed that one's fortune could be discovered in leaves. Interestingly, the Cumaean Sibyl had visions that she wrote down on leaves that she kept in her cave. As long as the leaves were undisturbed, they stayed in the correct order. But if someone opened the door to her cave and the winds blew in, the leaves were blown out of order. The prophetess did not sort the leaves and did not restore them to their correct order.

Oenone continued:

*"And them some gentle wind let blow abroad,*
*"[So] That all the world may see how false of love*
*"False Paris hath [has] to his Oenone been."*

The song ended, Oenone remained sitting.

Mercury said, "Good day, fair maiden. You are likely weary with the following of your game: the one you love. I wish thee the cunning ability to be able to spare or strike as you wish the one you love."

Oenone said, "I thank you, sir. My game — my prey, who is Paris — is quick, and clears a length of ground, and yet I am deceived, or else he has received a deadly wound."

She was punning on "quick," which meant both 1) alive and 2) fast.

Mercury said, "Your hand perhaps did move and your arrow went awry and so only wounded him."

"Or else it was my heart," Oenone said.

"Then surely he applied his footmanship and escaped by running quickly away from you," Mercury said.

"He played a ranging part," Oenone said.

Paris was a rover (one who ranged): 1) a wanderer in the woods and 2) a chaser after females other than Oenone.

"You should have given him a deeper wound," Mercury said.

"I could not do that because of pity," Oenone said.

"You should have eyed him better, then, so you could aim at him better," Mercury said.

"Blind love was not so witty," Oenone said.

"Why, tell me, sweet, are you in love?" Mercury asked.

"Oh, I wish I were not so," Oenone said.

"You mean because he does you wrong," Mercury said.

"Certainly, the more my woe," Oenone said.

"Why, do you mean Love, or him whom you loved?" Mercury asked.

Mercury was asking who wronged Oenone: the man she loved, or the Queen of Love?

"Well may I mean them both," Oenone said.

"Is love to blame?" Mercury asked.

"The Queen of Love has made him false to his vow," Oenone said.

"Do you mean, indeed, the Queen of Love?" Mercury asked.

"Yes, wanton Cupid's mother," Oenone said.

"Why, was thy love so lovely, then?" Mercury asked.

"His beauty is his shame," Oenone said. "He is the fairest shepherd on our green."

"Is he a shepherd, then?" Mercury asked.

"And for some time he kept a bleating flock," Oenone said.

"Enough, this is the man," Mercury said.

Mercury had been looking for Paris, and he had heard enough to know that Oenone was in love with Paris.

Mercury continued, "Where does he live, then?"

"About these woods, far from the poplar tree," Oenone said.

"What poplar tree do you mean?" Mercury asked.

"The poplar tree that is the witness of the vows between him and me," Oenone said. "Come and wend a little way, and you shall see his skill."

Paris' skill was carving false vows into a poplar tree.

"Sirs, stay here," Mercury said to the Cyclopes.

"No, let them go," Oenone said.

"No, not unless you will go," Mercury said. "Instead of going, stay, nymph, and listen to what I say about him thou so blame. Believe me, I have a sad discourse to tell thee before I go. Know then, my pretty lass, that I am named Mercury. I am the messenger of heaven, and I have flown hither to seize upon the man whom thou do love, to summon him before my father Jove, to answer a matter of great consequence. And know that Jove himself will not be long away from here."

Oenone replied, "Sweet Mercury, have poor Oenone's cries because of Paris' sin pierced the impartial skies and been heard by the unbiased gods?"

"The same is he, that jolly shepherd's swain," Mercury said.

Oenone described Paris: "His flock does graze upon the plain of Aurora, goddess of the dawn. The color of his coat is bright green. I wish that these eyes of mine had never seen his enticing curled hair, his ivory-white forehead. If I had not seen him, then I, poor I, would not have been made unhappy."

Mercury said, "It is no marvel, wench, that we cannot find him, when all too recently the Queen of Heaven is paying attention to him."

In this culture, the word "wench" was not negative.

The Queen of Heaven is Juno, who is married to Jupiter, the king of the gods. Because Paris had given the golden ball to Venus, Juno was angry at him. Because of that, Mercury thought that Venus might be keeping Paris out of sight.

Mercury continued, "But if thou will have medicine for thy sore, let others who wish to pay attention to him do so, but thou remember him no more. Find some other game — another man — and get thee gone. For here lusty suitors will come soon, too hot and lusty for thy dying vein. They are such as are never accustomed to make their suits in vain."

Jupiter and other gods — who were very successful in pursuing females and making them pregnant — were soon to arrive.

Mercury exited with the Cyclopes.

"I will go sit and pine under the poplar tree," Oenone said, "and I will write my answer to his vow, so that every eye may see it."

— 3.5 —

Venus, Paris, and the shepherds Hobbinol, Diggon, and Thenot talked together. The shepherds had told Venus about Colin's death, which had been caused by Thestylis not returning his love. Venus was carrying the golden ball that Paris had awarded to her.

As the Queen of Love, Venus usually wanted male lovers to be successful in their pursuit of females, and so she was upset by Thestylis' rejection of Colin and by his death.

"Shepherds," Venus said, "I am happy for this sweet shepherd's sake to take a strange revenge upon the maiden named Thestylis and her disdain. Let Colin's corpse be brought here now and buried in the plain. And let this be the inscription on his tomb:

"'*The love whom Thestylis has slain.*'

"And, trust me, I will chide my son for partiality, who gave the swain so deep a wound, and let her not be won by him."

"Alas, that ever Love was blind, to shoot so far amiss!" one of the shepherds said.

Cupid, god of love, had shot badly, causing Colin to fall in love with the wrong woman: a woman who did not return his love.

"Cupid my son was more to blame," Venus said. "The fault is not mine, but his."

The shepherds exited.

Paris said to Venus, "Oh, madam, if you yourself would condescend to perform the task of the handling of the bow, you yourself would have more skill and more justice than your son Cupid."

"Sweet shepherd, did thou ever love?" Venus asked.

"Lady, I loved a little once," Paris replied.

"And are thou changed?" Venus asked.

"Fair Queen of Love, I loved not all at once," Paris said.

He was able to love one female, and then love another. He was able to spread his love around.

"Well, wanton, if thou were wounded as deeply as some have been" — Venus may have been thinking of Colin the shepherd — "then it would take a cunning cure to heal your wound, and your wound would be rueful to be seen."

Paris asked, "But tell me, gracious goddess, for a start and false offence, does Venus or her son have the power at pleasure to give dispensation for it?"

Paris had started Oenone — made her come out of a place that ought to be safe — her innocence — and had made a false vow to her. Now he was wondering whether Venus and/or Cupid could forgive such an offence.

Venus replied:

"My boy, I will instruct thee with a piece of poetry

"That perhaps thou have not previously heard: In hell there is a tree,

"Where once a day do sleep the souls of false forsworn lovers,

"With open hearts; and there about in swarms the number hovers

"Of poor forsaken ghosts, whose wings from off this tree do beat

"Round drops of fiery Phlegethon [river of fire in hell] to scorch false hearts with heat.

"This pain did Venus and her son entreat the prince of hell

"To impose on such as were faithless to such as loved them well.

"And, therefore, this, my lovely boy, fair Venus does advise thee:

"Be true and steadfast in thy love, beware thou do disguise thee;"

In other words, don't lie (disguise your true self) when you say you love someone.

Venus continued:

"For he who makes love only a jest, when it pleases him to start [pursue a female],

"Shall feel those fiery water-drops consume his faithless heart."

In other words, be faithful in love, for if you are not, punishment in hell awaits you.

"Are Venus and her son so full of justice and severity?" Paris asked.

Venus said, "It would be a pity if love could not be linked with indifference. However lovers can cry out for hard success in love, trust me, some more than common cause that painful fortune does move."

According to Venus, although lovers cry for success in love — for the loved one to return their love — rejection affects the lover more strongly than would common cause, aka mutual love. Rejection can cause the lover to feel much more strongly than would acceptance.

We may wish that love not be linked with indifference — that is, we may wish that love should always be returned. For Venus, however, that would be a pity. She went on to explain that love linked with indifference is a very effective punishment.

Venus continued, "Cupid's bow is not alone his triumph, but his rod to punish people. Nor is he only just a boy, for he is called a mighty god. They who do him reverence have reason for the same: His shafts keep heaven and earth in awe, and shape 'rewards' for shame."

Cupid's arrows make people fall in love, but that love is not always returned. This shows Cupid's power: Not only can he make people very happy, but also he can make people very unhappy. As we have seen, Colin was so unhappy that he died. Cupid's arrows are so potent that they affect the immortals just as they do the mortals. When Cupid uses his arrows to punish people, the "rewards" he gives them are actually punishments.

Paris asked, "And has Cupid a reason to explain why Colin died for love?"

"Yes, he has a good reason, I promise thee, to explain why Colin's death might be necessary," Venus said.

"Then let the name of Love be adored," Paris said. "Cupid's bow is full of might."

Paris added, "Cupid's wounds are all but for desert and merit. Cupid's laws are all but right."

These sentences are ambiguous. The word "but" can mean 1) just, or 2) except. And so we have:

1) Paris added, "Cupid's wounds are all just for desert and merit. Cupid's laws are all just right."

2) Paris added, "Cupid's wounds are all except for desert and merit. Cupid's laws are all except right."

Venus said, "Well, for this once I wish to apply my speeches to thy sense, and Thestylis shall feel the pain for Love's supposed offence."

Venus believed that Paris wanted Thestylis to be punished for failing to return Colin's love, thus causing him to die of a broken heart.

The shepherds Hobbinol, Diggon, and Thenot brought in Colin's coffin on a bier, and then they sang a song titled "Welladay, Welladay," or "Alas, Alas":

*"Poor Colin, thou art [are] going to [into] the ground,*

*"The love whom Thestylis has slain,*

*"Hard heart, fair face, fraught [filled] with disdain,*

*"Disdain in love a deadly wound.*

*"Wound her, sweet Love, so deep again,*

*"[So] That she may feel the dying pain*

*"Of this unhappy shepherd's swain [Colin the unhappy lover and shepherd].*

*"And die for love as Colin died, as Colin died."*

Venus ordered, "Shepherds, pause. Let Colin's corpse be witness of the pain that Thestylis endures in love, a plague for her disdain. Behold the organ — the agent — of our wrath: This rusty churl is he. Thestylis dotes on his ill-favored — ugly — face, so much accursed is she.”

A wretched and deformed churl entered the scene. Thestylis, a pretty young woman, followed him and wooed him and sang to him a song titled “The Wooing of Colman,” but the churl rejected her and exited. Thestylis stayed behind.

Paris said, “Ah, poor unhappy Thestylis, unpitied is thy pain!”

Venus said, “Her fortune is not unlike hers whom thou cruelly has slain.”

Both Thestylis and Oenone suffered from the rejection of their love.

Thestylis sang and the shepherds sang and repeated some of the lyrics.

Thestylis sang:

*“The strange affects [passions] of my tormented heart,*

*“Whom cruel love has woeful prisoner caught,*

*“Whom cruel hate has into bondage brought,*

*“Whom wit [intelligence] no way of safe escape has taught,*

*“Enforce [Force] me [to] say, in witness of my smart [pain],*

*“There is no pain [comparable] to foul disdain in hardy suits of love.”*

The shepherds sang:

*“There is no pain [comparable] to foul disdain in hardy suits of love.”*

Thestylis sang:

*“Cruel, farewell.”*

The shepherds sang:

*“Cruel, farewell.”*

Thestylis sang:

*“Most cruel thou, of all that nature framed.”*

The shepherds sang, *“Most cruel thou, of all that nature framed.”*

Thestylis sang:

*“To kill thy love with thy disdain.”*

The shepherds sang:

*"To kill thy love with thy disdain."*
Thestylis sang:
*"Cruel, Disdain, so live thou named."*
The shepherds sang:
*"Cruel, Disdain, so live thou named."*
Thestylis sang:
*"And let me die of Iphis' pain."*
The shepherds sang:
*"A life too good for thy disdain."*
Thestylis sang:
*"Sith [Since] this my [astrological] stars to me allot,*
*"And thou thy love have all forgot."*
The shepherds sang:
*"And thou thy love have all forgot."*

In her song, Thestylis referred to Iphis, who loved the Cyprian maiden Anaxarete, who rejected his love. Iphis hanged himself after being rejected. Because Anaxarete showed no pity even when Iphis' funeral cortège passed by her, Venus turned her into stone.

After finishing her song, Thestylis exited.

Venus ordered, "Now, shepherds, bury Colin's corpse, perfume his coffin and bier with flowers, and record what justice Venus did amid these woods of yours."

The shepherds carried away Colin's coffin and bier.

Venus then said to Paris, "How are you now? How does my lovely boy feel after this mournful song about love?"

"Such mournful songs, sweet lady, as these, are deadly songs to experience," Paris said.

Seeing Mercury coming toward them, Venus said, "Cease, shepherd. There is other news coming, after this melancholy. My mind predicts some tempest coming with the speech of Mercury."

— **3.6** —

Mercury entered the scene, accompanied by some of Vulcan's Cyclopes.

Mercury said, "Fair Lady Venus, let me, who have long been well-beloved by thee, be pardoned, if, in accordance with my orders, I myself first bring to my sweet madam these unwelcome tidings."

"What news, what tidings, gentle Mercury, do you bring to trouble me in the midst of my delights?"

"At Juno's suit, Pallas assisting her, since both did join in appeal to Jupiter, a legal action has been entered in the court of heaven. And me, the swiftest of the seven planets, with a warrant they have thence dispatched away, to apprehend and find the man, they say, who gave away from them that self-same ball of gold that I presume I in this place behold."

We moderns know that the planet Mercury is the swiftest planet in the sense that its orbit around the Sun takes 88 Earth days.

Venus was holding the golden ball in her hands. Both Juno and Pallas believed that the golden ball did not belong to Venus.

Mercury continued, "That man, unless I am wide of the mark, is he who sits so near thy gracious side. This being so, it remains to be done that he leave here and appear before the gods to answer his offence."

"What tale is this?" Venus said. "Does Juno and her companion Pallas pursue this shepherd with such deadly hate as to say that they will not now be content with what was then our general agreement about how to award the golden ball?

"Let Juno strut, and let Pallas play her part. I won by merit what I have here. Both heaven and earth shall be brought to destruction, before wrong in this is done to Paris or me."

"This little fruit — this little golden apple — if Mercury can foretell the future, will send, I fear, a world of souls to hell," Mercury replied.

The Judgment of Paris led to the Trojan War. Many warriors on both sides died, and Troy — a center of civilization — fell.

"What mean these Cyclopes, Mercury?" Venus asked. "Has Vulcan grown so refined that he sends forth his chimney-sweepers to fetter any friend of mine?"

She then said to Paris, "Don't be downhearted by this, shepherd. I myself will be your bail."

Paris won't need to be arrested because Venus will guarantee his presence at the trial.

She then said to Mercury, "He shall be present at the court of Jove, I promise thee."

"Venus, give me your pledge," Mercury said.

The pledge would be a physical object that she would forfeit if Paris failed to show up for the trial.

Venus asked, "Do you want my cestus, or my fan, or both?"

A cestus is a marriage belt. Venus' marriage belt could make any male fall in lust with any female who wore it. During the Trojan War, Juno will borrow it in order to seduce her husband, Jupiter.

Mercury took her fan and said, "This shall serve. Your word to me is as sure as is your oath at Diana's bower. And, lady, if my intelligence or cunning may profit this man, for Venus' sake let him be bold enough to ask Mercury for help."

Mercury and the Cyclopes exited.

"Sweet Paris, what are you thinking about?"

Paris replied, "The angry heavens, because of this fatal jar — quarrel — name me as the cause of dire and deadly war."

# CHAPTER 4

**— 4.1 —**

Vulcan, the husband of Venus, was chasing one of Diana's nymphs in Diana's grove. Vulcan walked and ran with a limp.

"Why, nymph, for what reason do you need to run so fast? So what if I am dark and swarthy? I have more pretty knacks to please than every eye does see, and although I go not so upright, and although I am a blacksmith, to make me gracious you may have some other thing to make up for those things."

The "some other thing" may have been hanging in front below his waist.

"Knacks" are 1) tricks, or 2) trifles such as toys.

**— 4.2 —**

Bacchus, the god of wine, entered the scene and said, "Vulcan, will you act so indeed?"

He then said to the nymph, "Nay, turn, and tell him, girl, that he has a mistress — a wife — of his own to take his bellyful."

Vulcan had a thing below his waist that he used to fill female bellies.

Vulcan said, "Why, sir, if Phoebe's dainty nymphs please lusty Vulcan's tooth, why mayn't Vulcan tread awry as well as Venus does?"

Venus had affairs, and therefore, Vulcan was asking, why shouldn't he?

"You shall not taint your troth — break your marriage oath — for me," the nymph said. "You know very well that all who are Diana's maidens are vowed to halter apes into hell."

Diana, aka Phoebe, was a virgin goddess, and all the nymphs who served her were virgin maidens. In this culture, the lot of deceased old maids was to lead apes by the halter to hell.

The nymph meant that she intended to stay a virgin and serve Diana.

"Truly, truly, my gentle lass," Bacchus said, "but I do know a cast, lead apes who wishes, that we would help to unhalter them as fast."

A cast is a throw in wrestling. Bacchus knew a cast that would cast a nymph down on the ground where he could perform an act that would unhalter an ape and make it so that a nymph need not lead it.

As should be obvious, the male Olympian gods did not believe that the consent of the female was a necessary preliminary before having sex with her.

"For shame! For shame!" the nymph said to Bacchus.

She then said sarcastically, "Your skill is 'wondrously great'! I would have thought that the God of Wine would have just tended his tubs and grapes, and not been half so 'perfectly virtuous.'"

"Thank you for that quip, my girl," Vulcan said, appreciating the nymph's insulting Bacchus.

"That's one of a dainty nymph's sneers," Bacchus said.

The nymph said, "Please, sir, take it with all amiss — take it as the insult it was intended to be. We nymphs give out insults only after we have been given lumps — that is, been insulted or mistreated."

Vulcan said, "She has capped his answer in the Q."

The nymph was minding her Ps and Qs — she was on her best behavior. She had vowed to remain a virgin, and she was doing quite well in defending her virginity. In this case, being on her best behavior included arguing with and even insulting any god who wished to take her virginity.

The nymph asked, "What did Vulcan say? That the nymph has capped his answer in the Q?"

She then said to Vulcan, "She has done so as well as she who capped your head to keep you warm below."

According to the nymph, she had done as well at preventing Vulcan from sleeping with her as Venus had done. According to the nymph, Venus had put a nightcap on Vulcan's head to keep him warm below, rather than keeping warm what was below his waist by putting it in a warm, wet hole. Venus had also capped him with a cuckold's horns by being unfaithful to him, although this, of course, did not apply to the nymph.

Vulcan said, "Yes, then you will be shrewish, I see."

"It's best to leave her completely alone," Bacchus said.

"Yes, gentle gods, and find some other string to harp upon," the nymph said.

She meant this: Go find some other female to have sex with.

"Some other string!" Bacchus said. "Agreed, truly, some other pretty thing. It would be a shame for pretty maidens to be idle when they could be busy in bed.

"What do you say, nymph? Will you sing for us?"

"Yes, as long as the songs are some rounds or merry roundelays," the nymph said. "We sing no other songs: Your melancholic notes are not suitable for our country mirth."

Seeing Mercury and the Cyclopes coming, Vulcan said, "Here comes a crew who will help us sing."

— 4.3 —

Mercury and the Cyclopes entered the scene.

"Now our task is done," Mercury said.

Bacchus said, "Then, merry Mercury, it is more than time that this round were well begun."

They sang a song that began, "*Hey down, down, down.*"

When the song was finished, the nymph blew a horn loudly in Vulcan's ear and then ran away, giggling.

"She is a harlot, I promise," Vulcan said.

Bacchus said, "She is a peevish, elvish, spiteful, mischievous shrew."

Mercury said to Vulcan and Bacchus, "You could have seen as much of the nymph from far away as you have seen of her up close. Neither of you was successful at seeing her naked, for her kind of wandering was not the kind of wandering — philandering — you wanted.

"But, Bacchus, time spent with a nymph is well-spent time, I know."

He did not say that to Vulcan, perhaps because Vulcan was married to Venus, with whom Mercury had had an affair.

Mercury added, "Our sacred father — Jove — along with Phoebus Apollo and the God of War are meeting in Diana's grove."

Vulcan said, "Then we are here before the other gods yet: but wait, the earth is swelling. God Neptune, fortuitously, meets the prince of hell."

Pluto, the god of hell, sitting in his throne, ascended from below. Neptune also entered the scene.

Pluto asked, "What quarrels are these that call the gods of heaven and hell below?"

Neptune said, "It is a work of intelligence and toil to control a lusty shrew."

Jupiter's wife, Juno, was a shrewish wife.

— 4.4 —

Jupiter, Saturn, Apollo, Mars, Juno, Pallas, and Diana entered the scene.

In this trial, Juno and Pallas were the appellants, and nine male gods (including Jupiter) were the jury. Diana was attending because the trial was taking place in her grove — the woods around Mount Ida.

Jupiter was the chief judge, and Mercury carried out his orders.

Jupiter ordered, "Bring forth Paris, the man of Troy, so that he may hear for what reason he is to be arraigned before our court here."

Neptune said, "Look, he is coming, prepared to plead his case, escorted by lovely Venus, who shows him grace!"

Venus and Paris entered the scene.

Looking at Paris, Mercury said, "I have not seen a more alluring boy."

"So beauty is named the destruction of Priam's Troy," Apollo said.

The gods and the goddess Diana took their seats; Juno, Pallas, Venus, and Paris stood before them.

Venus said, "Sacred Jove, at Juno's arrogant, haughty complaint, as previously I gave my pledge to Mercury, I now bring the man whom he did recently summon, to answer his indictment orderly, and I crave this grace from this immortal senate: that you allow the mortal man to have an advocate to speak on his behalf."

Pallas said, "That may not be; the laws of heaven deny a man the grace to plead or answer by attorney."

"Pallas, thy judgment is all too peremptory," Venus said.

Apollo said, "Venus, that favor is flatly denied him. He is a mortal man, and therefore by our laws, he himself, without an advocate, must plead his own case."

Venus said to Paris, "Don't be dismayed, shepherd, in so good a case. Thou have friends, as well as foes, in this place."

Growing impatient, Juno asked, "Why, Mercury, why do you not indict him?"

"Speak softly, gentle Juno, please, do not bite him," Venus said.

"Gods, I trust that you are likely to have great silence, unless this parrot be commanded to leave hence," Juno said. "You gods won't be able to speak unless you order overly talkative Venus to go away from here."

Jupiter said, "Venus, forbear, be still."

He then ordered, "Speak, Mercury."

Venus said, "If Juno should jangle, prate, or babble, Venus will reply."

Mercury said, "Paris, King Priam's son, thou are accused of being partial and biased. You made a judgment that was partial and biased, and therefore unjust.

"Your accusers say that because you lacked impartiality, and because you completely ignored desert and merit, thou gave the prize to Lady Venus here and not to them.

"What is thine answer?"

Paris now made his oration to the Council of the Gods, defending himself and his decision.

He began by flattering the gods:

"Sacred and just, thou great and dread-inspiring Jove, and you thrice-revered powers, whom neither love nor hate of a person may wrest your judgments into being unjust, I address you.

"If my fate and fortune are that I, a mortal man, must plead for safe excusal of my guiltless thought, the great honor of pleading my case to a Council of the Gods makes my mishap the less."

Next, he pointed out that he was pleading for Venus — and her beauty — as well as for himself:

"I, a mortal man, must plead before the gods, who graciously tolerate the world's misdeeds, for Venus, but this heavenly council may with me affirm how enticing is her beauty.

"But since neither that nor this — neither my fate nor my fortune — may do me any good in providing an advocate for me, and therefore for myself I myself must be the speaker, a mortal man in the midst of this heavenly presence, then let me not create a long defense to them who are the beholders of my guiltless thoughts."

Actually, Paris would speak at length in his own defense.

Paris continued by saying that he did not deny the facts of the case — that he awarded the prize for beauty to Venus — but he pointed out that he is a mortal and that mortals sometimes err:

"I may not deny the deed that is all of my offence, but I do say that I did it upon command; if then I erred, I did no more than to a man belongs: To err is human.

"And if, in making a verdict on the three goddesses' divine forms, my dazzled eye did swerve or indulge more on Venus' face than on either face of the other two goddesses, it was no fault of bias or partiality, but instead, perhaps, the fault of a man whose eyesight was not so perfect as might discern the brightness of the rest."

In other words, his eyes could see the physical beauty of Venus but not the majesty of Juno or the wisdom of Athena.

Paris continued by saying that the male gods would also praise Venus' physical beauty:

"And, you gods, if it were permitted to men to know your secret thoughts, there are those who sit upon that sacred court who would with Paris err in Venus' praise.

"But let me cease to speak of error here, since what my hand, the organ of my heart, gave with the good agreement of my eye, my tongue is void with the task to maintain and defend in this court."

Paris was saying that his tongue was incapable of pleading in his defense. This is clearly wrong, just as Paris was wrong in saying earlier that he would not make a long defense. In both cases, he was engaging in false modesty and lowering expectations about the quality of defense he would make.

Pluto said, "He is a jolly shepherd, wise and eloquent."

Paris then pleaded innocent:

"First, then, accused of partiality, Paris replies, 'Not guilty of the fact.' His reason is that he knew no more fair Venus' marriage belt than Dame Juno's mace, and he never saw wise Pallas' crystal shield."

He had not seen the goddesses' special powers. Venus' marriage belt caused males to lust after females; since he had not seen and been affected by the marriage belt, he had not been biased by any effect it would have had on him. Juno's mace was a symbol of her majesty and power. Wise Pallas' shield was a symbol of her prowess in battle. Because he had not seen the goddesses' special powers, he had judged the three goddesses simply on their beauty, just as they had asked him to:

"Then as I looked, I loved and liked at once, and as making the judgment was referred from them to me, to give the prize to her whose beauty my fancy did best commend, so did I praise and judge as might my dazzled eyes discern."

Neptune said, "This is a piece of art, that cunningly, truly, refers the blame to the weakness of his eyes. Instead of Paris saying that he is to blame for any error, he is blaming the weakness of his eyes."

Paris continued with his defense:

"Now, because I must add justification for my deed and explain why Venus pleased me the most of the three, let me say first, in the twists and turns of my mortal ears, the question standing upon beauty's blaze, the goddess who is called the Queen of Love, I thought, should not be excelled in beauty.

"Had the prize been destined to be awarded to majesty — yet I will not rob Venus of her grace and prize — then stately Juno might have carried away the golden ball.

"Had the prize been dedicated to wisdom, my human wit would have given it to Pallas then.

"But since that power who threw the golden ball for my future ill did dedicate this ball to the fairest of the three goddesses, I thought the safest course of action was to judge on the basis of form and beauty rather than on the basis of Juno's stateliness or Pallas' worthiness.

"I used my shepherd's skill that learned to judge the fairest of the flock, and praised beauty only by nature's aim, and behold, Paris gave this fruit to Venus."

Paris then made the point that the three goddesses ought to accept his judgment, whether or not they agreed with it, because they themselves had chosen him to be their judge:

"I was a judge chosen there by the full consent of the three goddesses, and heavenly powers ought not to repent their deeds."

Paris then pointed out that each of the goddesses had offered him bribes to award her the golden ball and that therefore the goddesses themselves were not letting the contest be judged solely on which goddess was the fairest:

"Where it is said that beyond her deserving it, I honored Venus with this golden prize, you gods, alas, how can a mortal man discern among the sacred gifts of heaven?

"Or, if I may — with respect to you — let me reason thus: Suppose I gave, and judged corruptly then, out of hope of gaining that which did please my thought best, then this apple was not awarded for beauty's praise alone.

"I might offend in that way, since I was pardoned in advance with assurances that the three goddesses would accept my judgment, whatever it was.

"And I might offend in that way because I was tempted more than ever any creature was. I was tempted with wealth, with beauty, and with prowess in battle.

"I preferred beauty before them all; beauty is the thing that has enchanted heaven itself.

"As far as wealth is concerned, contentment is my wealth. A shell of salt will serve a shepherd swain, as will a small meal in a humble bag, and water running from the silver spring."

Possibly, shepherds near a coast scraped salt from a salt-encrusted seashell.

Paris continued, "As for weapons, they who sit so low dread no foes. A thorn bush can keep the wind from off my back. A thatched sheepcote is a shepherd's palace. The Muses tell epics of tragic war events; shepherds don't know the skill of telling epic tales. It is enough for shepherds, if Cupid has been displeased, to sing his praise by playing on a slender oaten pipe.

"And thus, thrice-revered gods and goddesses, I have told my tale, and I ask that any punishment of my guiltless soul be measured by my mind that did not intend any insult. If warlike Pallas or the Queen of Heaven sue to reverse my sentence by appeal, then let it be as pleases your divine majesties.

"The wrong and the hurt, if there will be any, will not be mine, but they will be hers whose beauty claimed the prize from me. If my decision to award the golden ball to Venus is reversed, it is Venus who will suffer the hurt."

Paris having ended his defense, Jupiter said, "Venus, take your shepherd away until he is called back to this place."

Venus and Paris exited.

Jupiter then said, "Juno, what can you do after hearing this defense but act justly and impartially? And if you will act justly in the case, you must recognize that the man must be acquitted by heaven's laws."

Juno disagreed: "Yes, gentle Jove, when Juno's suits are moved, then heaven may see how well she is beloved."

In other words, if the case goes against Juno and if Paris is acquitted, then all the gods and goddesses will know that Jupiter does not love her.

Apollo said to Juno, "But, madam, is it fitting for divine majesty to deviate in any way from justice?"

Pallas said, "Whether the man is guilty, yes or no, that does not hinder our appeal, I expect."

Whether Paris will be found guilty or not guilty of bias, Pallas still wanted his awarding of the golden ball to Venus to be overturned.

Juno said, "Phoebus Apollo, I know, amid this heavenly crew, there are those who have things to say as good as you."

She expected Apollo to support her — and then for other gods to agree with Apollo's support.

But Apollo did not support Juno.

He said, "And, Juno, I with them, and they with me, in law and right must necessarily agree."

Pallas said, "I grant that you may agree, but think carefully about that upon which you will agree."

Pluto said, "If you listened carefully, the man in his defense said what he said with reverence. He showed respect to all of us gods and goddesses."

"He showed respect to you goddesses very well, I promise you," Vulcan said.

"No doubt, sir, you say that cunningly," Juno, still angry, said.

"Well, Juno, if you will appeal, you may," Saturn, the god of agriculture, said. "But first let's finish the shepherd's case and send him away."

Mars said, "Upon appeal, Paris' judgment is likely to be overturned. Then Vulcan's wife is likely to have the wrong."

"And that in passion does to Mars belong," Juno said, referring to Mars' affair with Venus.

Jupiter ordered, "Call Venus and the shepherd in again."

Mercury exited to carry out the order.

"And set free the man so that he may know his pain," Bacchus said.

Apollo said, "His pain, his pain, his never-dying pain, a cause to make many more mortals complain."

The gods knew the fates of mortal men. They knew that Paris was fated to die during the Trojan War.

Mercury brought in Venus and Paris.

Jupiter said, "Shepherd, thou have been heard with equity and law, and because thy stars and fate draw thee to another situation, we here dismiss thee from here, by order of our senate. Go make thy way to Troy, and there await thy fate."

Jupiter did not say what Paris' fate was; he said only that Paris had a different fate than being judged by the Council of Gods.

"Sweet shepherd, you go with such luck in love, while thou do live, as may the Queen of Love to any lover give," Venus said.

Venus would keep her promise to give Helen to Paris.

"My luck is loss, however my love does succeed," Paris said. "I am afraid that I, Paris, shall only rue my deed."

Jupiter had not said that Paris' fate was bad, but Paris could guess that the consequences of taking Helen away from her husband would be bad.

Paris exited.

"From the woods of Ida now wends the shepherd's boy who in his bosom carries fire to Troy," Apollo said.

As a god, Apollo knew that the Trojan War would end with Troy in flames.

Paris had been disposed of, but there was still the question of whether to allow his awarding of the golden ball to Venus to stand. Juno and Pallas were appealing Paris' verdict.

"Venus, these ladies do appeal, you see," Jupiter said. "And the gods agree that they may appeal. It rests, then, that you be well content to stand in this appeal until our final judgment; if King Priam's son did well in this, then the law of heaven will not lead amiss. If Paris rightly awarded you the golden ball, then no injustice will occur in the gods' decision."

Venus replied, "But, sacred Jupiter, if I, thy daughter, might choose, she — that is, I — might with reason refuse this appeal: Yet, if Juno and Pallas are unmoved when they should feel shame, let it be a stain and blemish to their names. Let it be a deed, too, far unworthy of the place, unworthy Pallas' lance, or Juno's mace. But if to beauty the golden ball shall be bequeathed, I don't doubt but it will return to me."

She lay down the ball.

"Venus, there is no more ado than so: The golden ball rests where the gods do it bestow," Pallas said.

Neptune said, "But, ladies, because of your rage, however our decision comes out, you have the advantage."

No matter which goddess is awarded the golden ball, the other two goddesses will be angry. In addition, even the winning goddess may be angry at a god who argued unsuccessfully for another goddess to win the golden ball. Because of the goddesses' anger, the gods are unlikely to speak what they feel is the truth, the whole truth, and nothing but the truth in their presence.

Jupiter said, "Then, dames, so that we gods more freely may debate, and hear the fair and impartial sentence of this senate, you goddesses withdraw yourselves from this presence for a space, until we have thoroughly discussed the case. Diana shall be your guide; nor shall you yourselves need to inquire how things turn out here. We will, when we resolve the situation, let you know how everything turns out in accordance with our general judgment."

Diana said to Jupiter, "Thy will is my wish. What you want me to do is what I want to do."

She then said to the three goddesses, "Fair ladies, will you leave now?"

"Curse her whom this sentence does offend," Juno said.

She would be offended if she were not awarded the golden ball, and she would not curse herself, and so Juno was saying that she expected to be awarded the golden ball.

Venus said, "Now, Jove, be just; and, gods, you who are Venus' friends, if you have ever done her wrong, then now may you make amends."

Venus, of course, wanted to be awarded the golden apple.

Pallas, of course, also wanted to be awarded the golden apple, but as the goddess of wisdom, she did not now say something in order to influence the judges.

Diana, Juno, Pallas, and Venus exited.

"Venus is fair, and Pallas and Juno are fair, too," Jupiter said. "All of them are beautiful."

"But tell me now without some more trouble and ado," Vulcan said, "who is the fairest woman, and do not flatter that she."

Because Venus was his wife and because Venus was objectively the most physically beautiful of the three goddesses, Vulcan wanted Venus to be awarded the golden ball.

Pluto said, "Vulcan, all the matter hangs upon comparison. That done, the quarrel and the strife will be ended."

Wrong. The quarrel and the strife will not be ended. No matter which goddess they choose to award the golden ball, two goddesses will be insulted and angry.

"Because it is known which goddess is physically the most beautiful, the quarrel is pretended," Mars said. "The comparison has already been made in our minds."

Vulcan said, "Mars, you have reason for your speech, certainly. My dame, I know, is fairest in your eye."

No doubt; after all, Mars and Venus had had an affair.

"If I did not think that she is the fairest," Mars replied, "I would be doing her a double wrong."

He would be doing her wrong as her judge and as her lover.

Saturn said, "We tarry here so long about what is only a trifle. Let's vote: Give it by voices, and let voices give the odds. This is such a trifle that troubles all the gods!"

Neptune said, "Believe me, Saturn. I agree with you."

Bacchus said, "Let's take a vote."

Pluto said, "Let's take a vote."

Bacchus said, "Let's take a vote, if Jove agrees."

"Gentle gods, I am neutral," Mercury said. "But then I know who's likely to be criticized."

Jupiter was the god who is likely to be criticized. Venus is objectively the most physically beautiful, but if Juno — who is a shrewish wife to Jupiter — loses, she will greatly criticize her husband, who is one of the judges.

Apollo said, "Thrice-revered gods, and thou, immortal Jove, if Phoebus Apollo may, as is very much his due according to our laws, be licensed to speak uprightly in this uncertain and fearsome case (since women's wits work to create unceasing woes for men), then let me say this:

"To make the three goddesses friends — the goddesses who now are friendless foes because each has claimed the golden ball — and to keep peace with them, with us, and all, let us refer this sentence — this judgment — to where it does belong.

"Please don't think, you gods, that my speech takes away from the sacred power of this immortal senate because I recommend a change in this case's judges.

"In this case, I say, fair Phoebe — Diana — has been wronged.

"I don't mean that her beauty should bear away the prize, but instead I mean that the holy law of heaven does not allow for one god to meddle in another's power.

"Because the Judgment of Paris befell so near Diana's bower, she is the fittest judge in my opinion for appeasing this unpleasant grudge. Let us allow her to award the golden ball."

Apollo was pointing out that the gods and goddesses had their own domains, and it was forbidden for the gods and goddesses to interfere in others' domains. Since the Judgment of Paris took place in Diana's domain, she ought to be the judge: She had jurisdiction in this case.

Apollo gave some examples of non-inference in others' domains:

"If Jove does not exercise power in Pluto's hell with charms, if Mars has the sovereign power to manage arms, if Bacchus bears no rule in Neptune's sea, if Vulcan's fire does not obey Saturn's scythe because Vulcan and not Saturn is fire's master, then let us not suppress, against law and equity, Diana's power in her own territory. Diana's rule, amid her sacred bowers on Mount Ida, is as properly recognized as any rule of yours.

"By turning over the judgment to Diana, we may wipe all the court's speech away so well that Pallas, Juno, and Venus have to say and recognize that by the justice of our laws we were not allowed to judge and conclude the case. And this appears to me the most egalitarian judgment: A woman will be the judge among her peers."

Mercury said, "Apollo has discovered the only way to completely rid us of the blame and trouble of making the judgment."

"We are beholden to his sacred wit," Vulcan said.

"I can praise and well allow Apollo's recommendation," Jupiter said. "By letting Diana have the giving of the ball, we will divert the matter from us all."

Vulcan said, "If we do this, Jove may clearly excuse himself from the case, where Juno otherwise would chide him and brawl with him quickly apace."

The gods stood up.

Mercury said, "And now it would take some cunning to divine to whom Diana will this prize resign. It will take a wise god to guess to whom Diana will award the golden ball."

"It is enough for me that I won't have to participate in making that decision," Vulcan said.

Bacchus joked, "Vulcan, although thou are black with soot from blacksmithing and are ugly, thou are not at all refined."

Vulcan joked back, "Go bathe thyself, Bacchus, in a tub of wine. The ball's as likely to be mine as thine. Neither of us is good-looking."

# CHAPTER 5

— 5.1 —

Diana, Juno, Pallas, and Venus talked together.

Diana said, "Ladies, far beyond what I hoped for and wanted, you see, this thankless task is imposed on me; if you will rest as well content as Diana will be an impartial judge, my fair decision shall none of you offend, and we will of this quarrel make a final end.

"Therefore, whether you are eager or reluctant, confirm your promise with some sacred oath."

Pallas said, "Phoebe, chief mistress of this game-filled woods, you whom the gods have chosen to conclude the case that in balance yet lies undecided, concerning the bestowing of this golden prize, I give my promise and my oath:

"By the Styx, by heaven's imperial power, by all that belongs to Pallas' deity — her shield, her lance, her battle ensigns, her sacred wreath of olive and of laurel, her crested helmet, and whatever else Pallas may possess — I swear that wherever this ball of purest gold, that chaste Diana here in her hand does hold, impartially her wisdom shall bestow, Pallas shall rest content and satisfied without any more dislike or quarrel and say that the one who best deserves the golden ball is the one who wins it."

An oath that is sworn by the Styx, a river in the Land of the Dead, is an inviolable oath.

Juno said, "And here I promise and profess this:

"That by the Styx, by heaven's imperial power, by all that belongs to Juno's deity — her crown, her mace, her ensigns of majesty, her spotless and chaste marriage-rites, her divine league, and by that holy name of Proserpine — I swear that wherever this ball of purest gold, that chaste Diana here in her hand does hold, impartially her wisdom shall bestow, Juno shall rest content and satisfied without any more dislike or quarrel and say that the one who best deserves the golden ball is the one who wins it."

Venus said, "And, lovely Phoebe, because I know your judgment will be no other than shall become thee, behold, I take thy dainty hand to kiss, and with my solemn oath confirm my promise:

"That by the Styx, by Jove's immortal power and domain, by Cupid's bow, by Venus' myrtle-tree, by Vulcan's gifts of my marriage belt and my fan, by this red rose, whose red color first began when formerly my wanton boy Cupid (the more his blame) did draw his bow awry and hurt his dame — me — and made her bleed on a white rose, by all the honor and the sacrifice that from the island of Cithaeron and from the coastal city of Paphos rise, I swear that wherever this ball of purest gold, that chaste Diana here in her hand does hold, impartially her wisdom shall bestow, Venus shall rest content and satisfied without any more dislike or quarrel and say that the one who best deserves the golden ball is the one who wins it."

Diana now described a nymph named Eliza. Remarkably, much that she and others would say about Eliza could be said about Queen Elizabeth I of England, who would rule many hundreds of years later.

Diana said, "Your vows are what were needed, and so, goddesses, listen carefully.

"Within these pleasant shady woods, where neither storm nor sun's distemperature have the power to hurt by cruel heat or cold, under the climate of the mild heaven ...

"Where seldom Jove's angry thunderbolt lights and lands, because he favors that sovereign earthly peer who lives there ...

"Where whistling winds make music among the trees — far from disturbance of our country gods, amid the cypress-springs ...

"There lives a gracious nymph who honors Diana for her chastity, and likes well the labors of Phoebe's groves.

"The place is called Elysium, and the name of the woman who governs there is Eliza."

Elysium is the name of the pleasant place in the Land of the Dead where virtuous souls go.

Diana continued, "It is a kingdom that may well compare with mine. It is an ancient seat of kings, a second Troy, encompassed round with a beneficial, commodious sea."

A sea surrounds and protects England just as high walls for a long time protected Troy. In addition, a man named Brute of Troy who was a descendant of the Trojan Aeneas was believed to have settled in Britain.

Diana continued, "Her people are called Angeli. Or, if I am mistaken, I am at most mistaken by only a letter."

*Angeli* is Latin for "angels," but Diana had meant — unless she had made the flattering mistake on purpose — to refer to the Angles who settled in England with the Saxons and Jutes. Many English citizens are Anglo-Saxons.

Diana continued, "Eliza gives laws of justice and of peace, and on her head, as befits her fortune best, she wears a wreath of laurel, gold, and palm. Her robes are dyed purple and scarlet. Her veil is white, as best befits a maiden."

Queen Elizabeth I was known as the Virgin Queen; she never married. Both Diana and Pallas Athena were virgin goddesses.

Diana continued, "Her ancestors live in the House of Fame."

Some of Queen Elizabeth I's ancestors were buried in Westminster Abbey.

Diana continued, "She gives arms of happy victory, and flowers to deck her lions crowned with gold."

The lion is a symbol of England.

Diana continued, "This peerless nymph, whom both heaven and earth love, this sole paragon, is she in whom so many gifts in one do meet and on whom our country gods so often gaze, and in honor of whose name the Muses sing.

"In state she is Queen Juno's peer, for power in arms and virtues of the mind she is Minerva's — Pallas Athena's — mate, she is as fair and lovely as the Queen of Love, and she is as chaste as Diana in her chaste desires.

"The same is she, if Phoebe — I, Diana — does no wrong, to whom this ball by merit does belong."

Pallas said, "If this be she whom some Zabeta call, to whom thy wisdom well bequeaths the ball, I can remember how Flora with her flowers strewed the earth at Zabeta's day of birth and how every power with heavenly majesty in person honored that occasion of celebration."

"Zabeta" is a variation of the end of "Elizabeth." "Eliza Zabeta" is much like "Elizabeth."

Juno said, "The lovely Graces were not far away. They threw their balm for joy on that day."

Venus said, "The Fates against their nature began a cheerful song, and with favor vowed to prolong her life."

The three Fates are Clotho, Lachesis, and Atropos. Clotho spins the thread of life. Lachesis measures the thread of life, determining how long a person lived. Atropos cuts the thread of life; when the thread is cut, the person dies.

The three Fates are more concerned with ending life than prolonging it, but the three Fates decided to gift Eliza with a long life.

Venus continued, "Then Cupid's eyesight first began to grow dim. Probably Eliza's beauty blinded him. To this fair nymph, who is not earthly but divine, I am happy to give the golden ball."

Pallas said, "To this fair queen, so beautiful and wise, Pallas bequeaths her title in the prize."

Juno said, "To her whom Juno's looks so well become, the Queen of Heaven yields to Phoebe's — Diana's — decision. And I am glad Diana found the skill to please desert and merit so well without offence."

Diana said, "Then listen carefully to my tale. The usual time is nigh when the Dames of Life and Destiny — the three Fates — dressed in robes of cheerful colors, are accustomed to come to this renowned queen who is so wise and fair and to greet with pleasant songs this peerless nymph.

"Clotho lays down her distaff — the rod on which thread is spun — at her feet.

"And Lachesis pulls the thread and makes it long.

"The third — Atropos — with favor gives the thread size and strength, and contrary to her cutting the thread gives Eliza permission to weave her web of life as she likes best.

"This time of greeting we will attend, and in the meanwhile charm away the tediousness of waiting with some sweet song."

Music sounded, and the Nymphs sang and played musical instruments.

The goddesses did not have to wait long, for the three Fates — Clotho, Lachesis, and Atropos — soon appeared and drew a curtain and began singing near a chair of state on which Eliza was sitting. The three Fates regarded Eliza as a Queen.

Clotho sang:

"*Humanae vitae filum sic volvere Parcae.*"

["So the Fates spin the thread of human life."]

Lachesis sang:

"*Humanae vitae filum sic tendere Parcae.*"

["So the Fates draw the thread of human life."]

Atropos sang:

"*Humanae vitae filum sic scindere Parcae.*"

["So the Fates cut the thread of human life."]

Clotho sang:

"*Clotho colum bajulat.*"

["Clotho bears the distaff."]

Lachesis sang:

"*Lachesis trahit.*"

["Lachesis measures."]

Atropos sang:

"*Atropos occat.*"

["Atropos cuts."]

The three Fates sang together:

"*Vive diu foelix votis hominúmque deúmque,*

"*Corpore, mente, libro, doctissima, candida, casta.*"

["Live long blest with the gifts of men and gods,

["In body and mind free, wisest, pure and chaste."]

As they sang the next few lines, the three Fates then lay down at the Queen's feet the items that they were holding.

Clotho sang:

"*Clotho colum pedibus.*"

["Clotho her distaff (lays) at your feet."]

Lachesis sang:

"*Lachesis tibi pendula fila.*"

["Lachesis (gives) to you her hanging thread."]

She was referring to a spindle and reel.

Atropos sang:

"*Et fatale tuis manibus ferrum Atropos offert.*"

["Atropos offers to your hands her far fate-enclosing steel."]

Her far fate-enclosing steel is a knife for cutting the thread of life.

The three Fates sang together:

"*Vive diu foelix votis hominúmque deúmque,*

"*Corpore, mente, libro, doctissima, candida, casta.*"

["Live long blest with the gifts of men and gods,

["In body and mind free, wisest, pure and chaste."]

Once the three Fates finished singing the song, Clotho said to the Queen, "Gracious and wise, fair Queen of rare renown and fame, whom heaven and earth love, amid thy retinue, noble and lovely peers, to honor thee, and do thee favor more than may belong by nature's law to any earthly mortal, witness the continuance of our yearly tribute to you. We impartial Dames of Destiny meet, as the gods and we have agreed in one, in reverence of Eliza's noble name.

"And, look, Clotho humbly yields her distaff!"

Lachesis said, "Her spindle and her fate-dealing reel, Lachesis lays down in reverence at Eliza's feet.

"*Te tamen in terris unam tria numina*

"*Divam Invita statuunt natura lege sorores,*

"*Et tibi non aliis didicerunt parcere Parcoe.*"

["The three sisters, despite the law of nature,

["Appoint thee a goddess unique, though on earth;

["And thee and no other have the Fates learned to spare."]

Atropos said, "Dame Atropos, just as her partners have done, to thee, fair Queen, resigns her fate-dealing knife.

"Live long the noble phoenix of our age, our fair Eliza, our fair Zabeta!"

Diana said, "And, look, in addition to this rare and splendid celebration and this sacrifice these dames are accustomed to do, which is a favor much indeed against the three Fates' natures, this prize from heaven and heavenly goddesses is bequeathed unto thy worthiness!"

She put the golden ball into Eliza's — or Queen Elizabeth I's — own hands.

(George Peele's play was performed before Queen Elizabeth I.)

Diana continued, "Accept it, then. It is thy due by Diana's judgment, which is praise of the wisdom, the beauty, and the majestic stateliness that best become thy peerless excellency."

Venus said, "So, fair Eliza, Venus does resign the honor of this honor because this honor is thine."

Juno said, "So also is the Queen of Heaven content likewise to yield to thee her title in the prize."

Pallas said, "So Pallas yields the praise hereof to thee because of thy wisdom, princely state, and peerless beauty."

# EPILOGUE

Everybody sang this song:
   "*Vive diu felix votis hominumque deumque,*
   "*Corpore, mente, libro, doctissima, candida, casta.*"
   ["Live long and happy with the gifts of men and gods,
   ["In body and mind free, wisest and most learned, pure, and chaste."]

# NOTES

— 2.1 —

Juno says this:

> *My face is fair; but yet the majesty,*
> *That all the gods in heaven have seen in me,*
> *Have made them choose me, of the planets seven.*

***

The seven planets known to the Elizabethans include five that were named after gods: Mercury, Venus, Mars, Jupiter, and Saturn; the Elizabethans also considered the Moon and Sun to be planets. They believed that the Sun orbited the Earth.

Juno, in fact, was associated with the Moon.

***

The below is from the Wikipedia article on "Hera" in the section titled "Youth":

*Hera was also worshipped as a virgin: there was a tradition in Stymphalia in Arcadia that there had been a triple shrine to Hera the Girl (Παις [Pais]), the Adult Woman (Τέλεια [Teleia]), and the Separated (Χήρη [Chérē] 'Widowed' or 'Divorced'). In the region around Argos, the temple of Hera in Hermione near Argos was to Hera the Virgin. At the spring of Kanathos, close to Nauplia, Hera renewed her virginity annually, in rites that were not to be spoken of (arrheton). The Female figure, showing her "Moon" over the lake is also appropriate, as Hebe[1], Hera, and Hecate; new moon, full moon, and old moon in that order and otherwise personified as the Virgin of Spring, The Mother of Summer, and the destroying Crone of Autumn.*

---

1.　　*https://en.wikipedia.org/wiki/Hebe_(mythology)*

Source: "Hera." Wikipedia. Accessed on 18 May 2019 <https://en.wikipedia.org/wiki/Hera>.

***

The below information comes from the entry on "Juno" in *Encyclopedia of Goddesses and Heroines: Europe and the Americas*:

*A temple devoted to Juno on the Mons Cispius, whose sacred trees were planted before Rome was built, suggests that Juno was older than the city. Similarly, the cult of Juno on the Capitoline Hill appears to antedate Rome. What Juno represented to her original worshipers is difficult to determine. Attempts to translate her name's meaning have been inconclusive, but it appears related to "light," an interpretation supported by the titles Lucina ("light") and Caelistis ("sky"). For this reason, and because she was honored on new moons, Juno has been interpreted as a moon goddess. But Juno has also been connected with the gate god Janus, both representing passage from one state to another; she may have originally been called Jana.*

Source: Patricia Monaghan, "Juno." *Encyclopedia of Goddesses and Heroines: Europe and the Americas*. P. 456.

***

The below information comes from C.M.C. Green, *Roman Religion and the Cult of Diana at Aricia*:

*[Birt] was quite correct that other deities (not just goddesses) were in fact associated with the moon: Juno, for instance, has been identified as a moon goddess.*

Source: C.M.C. Green, *Roman Religion and the Cult of Diana at Aricia* (Cambridge University Press, 2007), p. 73.

***

The below information comes from the Wikipedia article on "Luna (goddess)":

*Luna is not always a distinct goddess, but sometimes rather an epithet that specializes a goddess, since both Diana and Juno are identified as moon goddesses.[1]*[2]

*1) C.M.C. Green, Roman Religion and the Cult of Diana at Aricia (Cambridge University Press, 2007), p. 73.*

Source: "Luna (goddess)." Wikipedia. Accessed on 18 May 2019 <https://en.wikipedia.org/wiki/Luna_(goddess)>.

The below information comes from the GreekGods.org article on "Phoebe (Phoibe)," which also provides information on why Diana is also called Phoebe:

*Phoebe was a Titan goddess of prophetic radiance, often associated with Selene (goddess of the moon). She, however, had never been referred as the goddess of the moon. The misinterpretation probably comes because her granddaughter Artemis was also called Phoebe, after her, just like her grandson Apollo was called Phoebus. And latin authors were all referring Phoebe as the moon goddess or moon itself, but they clearly had Artemis in mind doing so. That is why the Titaness is often misidentified as the moon goddess. To the Greeks it was pretty simple and obvious that Selene was the correct goddess. Romans on the other hand associated Artemis, Hera[3] and Selene to the moon amongst others, but there was no mentioning of Titaness Phoebe. However, some researchers believe that Artemis (Diana, Phoebe) became known as the goddess of the moon because of her grandmother whom she got the name after. Anyhow, Phoebe was rather associated with being prophetic, like her sister Themis and her mother Gaea. She was also one of the twelve titans who were the descendants of Uranus and Gaea. She was, like all of her sisters, never involved in the war between Titans and Olympian gods, and was spared from being imprisoned in Tartarus. Instead, she took her place at the oracle of Delphi.*

---

2.　　　*https://en.wikipedia.org/wiki/Luna_(goddess)#cite_note-1*

3.　　　*https://www.greek-gods.org/olympian-gods/hera.php*

Source: "Phoebe (Phoibe)." GreekGods.org. Accessed on 31 May 2019. <https://tinyurl.com/y5t6xuhz>.

— 2.2 —

The English translation of Helen's Italian song comes from the following source:

Morley, Henry. *English Plays*. London: Cassell, Petter, Galpin & Co. (no date).

— 3.2 —

Thenot says this:

*Lo, yonder comes the lovely nymph, that in these Ida vales*
*Plays with Amyntas' lusty boy, and coys him in the dales!*


***


Who is Amyntas? The best answer that I can come up with is that *Amyntas* is an error for *Agelaus*.


***


The below information comes from the Wikipedia article titled "Paris (mythology)":

*Paris was a child of Priam and Hecuba (see the list of King Priam's children). Just before his birth, his mother dreamed that she gave birth to a flaming torch. This dream was interpreted by the seer Aesacus as a foretelling of the downfall of Troy, and he declared that the child would be the ruin of his homeland. On the day of Paris's birth, it was further announced by Aesacus that the child born of a royal Trojan that day would have to be killed to spare the kingdom, being the child that would bring about the prophecy. Though Paris was indeed born before nightfall, he was spared by Priam. Hecuba was also unable to kill the child, despite the urging of the priestess of Apollo, one Herophile. Instead, Paris's father prevailed upon his chief herdsman, Agelaus, to remove the child and kill him. The herdsman, unable to use a weapon against the infant, left him exposed on Mount Ida, hoping he would perish there (cf. Oedipus). He was, however, suckled by a she-bear. Returning after nine days, Agelaus was astonished to find the child still alive and brought him home in a backpack (Greek[4] pḗra, hence by folk etymology Paris's name) to rear as his own. He returned to Priam bearing a dog's tongue as evidence of the deed's completion.*

Source: "Paris (mythology)." Wikipedia. Accessed on 19 May 2019 <https://en.wikipedia.org/wiki/Paris_(mythology)>.

— 5.1 —

The English translation of the three Fates' Latin song comes from the following source:

Morley, Henry. *English Plays*. London: Cassell, Petter, Galpin & Co. (no date).

Note: Two lines of the song also appear in the Epilogue.

***

The English translation of Lachesis' Latin words (after the three Fates' song) comes from the following source: Baskerville, Charles Read, et al. editors. *Elizabethan and Stuart Plays*. New York: Holt, Rinehart and Winston, 1934.

---

4.    https://en.wikipedia.org/wiki/Ancient_Greek

# APPENDIX A: BACKGROUND INFORMATION

**• What is the basic story of the Trojan War?**

Paris, prince of Troy, visits Menelaus, king of Sparta, and then Paris runs off with Menelaus' wife, Helen, who of course becomes known as Helen of Troy. This is a major insult to Menelaus and his family, so he and his older brother, Agamemnon, lead an army against Troy to get Helen (and Menelaus' treasure that Paris also stole) back. The war drags on for ten years, and the greatest Greek warrior is Achilles, while the greatest Trojan warrior is Hector, Paris' oldest brother. Eventually, Hector is killed by Achilles, who is then killed by (Apollo and) Paris, who is then killed by Philoctetes. Finally, Odysseus comes up with the idea of the Trojan Horse, which ends the Trojan War.

**• Who is Achilles, and what is unusual about his mother, Thetis?**

Achilles, of course, is the foremost warrior of the Greeks during the Trojan War. His mother, Thetis, is unusual in that she is a goddess. The Greeks' religion was different from many modern religions in that the Greeks were polytheistic (believing in many gods) rather than monotheistic (believing in one god). In addition, the gods and human beings could mate and have children. Achilles is unusual in that he had an immortal goddess as his mother and a mortal man, Peleus, as his father.

**• What prophecy was made about Thetis' male offspring?**

The prophecy about Thetis' male offspring was that he would be a greater man than his father. This is something that would make most human fathers happy. (One exception would be Pap, a character in Mark Twain's *Adventures of Huckleberry Finn*. Pap does not want Huck, his son, to learn to read or write or to get an education or to live better than Pap does.)

**• Who is Jupiter, and what does he decide to do as a result of this prophecy?**

Jupiter is a horny god who sleeps with many goddesses and many human beings. Normally, he would lust after Thetis, but once he hears the prophecy about her, he does not want to sleep with Thetis. For one thing, the gods are potent, and when they mate they have children. Jupiter overthrew his own father, and Jupiter does not want Thetis to give birth to a greater man than he is because his son will overthrow him. Therefore, Jupiter wants to get Thetis married off to someone else. In this case, a marriage to a human being for Thetis would suit Jupiter just fine. A human son may be greater than his father, but he is still not going to be as great as a god, and so Jupiter will be safe if Thetis gives birth to a human son.

**• Who is Peleus?**

Peleus is the human man who marries Thetis and who fathers Achilles. At the time of Homer's *Iliad*, Peleus is an old man and Thetis has not lived with him for a long time.

**• Why is Eris, goddess of discord, not invited to the wedding feast of Peleus and Thetis?**

Obviously, you do not want discord at a wedding, and therefore, Eris, goddess of discord, is not invited to the wedding feast of Peleus and Thetis. Even though Eris is not invited to the wedding feast, she shows up anyway.

Note: In George Peele's play *The Arraignment of Paris*, it is the goddess Até who shows up with the golden apple.

**• Eris, goddess of discord, throws a golden apple on a table at the wedding feast. What is inscribed on the golden apple?**

Inscribed on the golden apple is the phrase "For the fairest," written in Greek. Because Greek is a language that indicates masculine and feminine in certain words, and since "fairest" has a feminine ending, the golden apple is really inscribed "for the fairest female."

Note: In George Peele's play *The Arraignment of Paris*, it is the goddess Até who shows up with the golden apple.

 • **Juno, Pallas, and Venus each claim the apple. Who are they?**

Three goddesses claim the apple, meaning that each of the three goddesses thinks that she is the fairest, or most beautiful.

*Juno*

Juno is the wife of Jupiter, and she is a jealous wife. Jupiter has many affairs with both immortal goddesses and mortal women, and Juno is jealous because of these affairs. Jupiter would like to keep on her good side.

*Pallas*

Pallas is the goddess of wisdom. She becomes the patron goddess of Athens. Pallas especially likes Odysseus, as we especially see in Homer's *Odyssey*. Pallas is a favorite of Jupiter, her father. Jupiter would like to keep on her good side.

*Venus*

Venus is the goddess of sexual passion. She can make Jupiter fall in love against his will. Jupiter would like to keep on her good side.

*Roman Gods and Goddesses*

The Greek gods and goddesses have Roman equivalents. The Roman name is followed by the Greek name:

Apollo: Apollo (same name)

Diana: Artemis

Juno: Hera

Jupiter: Zeus

Mars: Ares

Mercury: Hermes

Minerva: Pallas Athena

Neptune: Poseidon

Pluto: Hades

Venus: Aphrodite

Vulcan: Hephaestus

- **Why doesn't Jupiter want to judge the goddesses' beauty contest?**

Jupiter is not a fool. He knows that if he judges the goddesses' beauty contest, he will make two enemies. The two goddesses whom Jupiter does not choose as the fairest will hate him and likely make trouble for him.

Please note that the Greek gods and goddesses are not omnibenevolent. Frequently, they are quarrelsome and petty.

By the way, Athens, Ohio, lawyer Thomas Hodson once judged a beauty contest featuring 25 cute child contestants. He was running in an election to choose the municipal court judge, and he thought that judging the contest would be a good way to win votes. Very quickly, he decided never to judge a children's beauty contest again. He figured out that he had won two votes — the votes of the parents of the child who won the contest. Unfortunately, he also figured out that he had lost 48 votes — the votes of the parents of the children who lost.

- **Who is Paris, and what is the Judgment of Paris?**

Paris is a prince of Troy, and Jupiter allows him to judge the three goddesses' beauty contest. Paris is not as intelligent as Jupiter, or he would try to find a way out of judging the beauty contest.

- **Each of the goddesses offers Paris a bribe if he will choose her. What are the bribes?**

*Juno*

Juno offers Paris political power: several cities he can rule.

*Pallas*

Pallas offers Paris prowess in battle. Paris can become a mighty and feared warrior.

*Venus*

Venus offers Paris the most beautiful woman in the world to be his wife.

- **Which goddess does Paris choose?**

Paris choses Venus, who offered him the most beautiful woman in the world to be his wife.

**How much of the Trojan War is covered in George's Peele's *The Arraignment of Paris*?**

The Judgment of Paris appears in George Peele's play; in addition, the play has a trial in which the male Olympian gods judge whether Paris is guilty of bias in awarding the golden apple to Venus. However, at the end of the play, Paris has not yet run away with Helen, and the Trojan War has not yet started.

Nevertheless, it is important to know this background information to fully understand the play.

**Note**

I have used information presented in Elizabeth Vandiver's course on the *Iliad*, which is available from the Teaching Company, in this section titled "Background Information."

# APPENDIX B: ABOUT THE AUTHOR

It was a dark and stormy night. Suddenly a cry rang out, and on a hot summer night in 1954, Josephine, wife of Carl Bruce, gave birth to a boy — me. Unfortunately, this young married couple allowed Reuben Saturday, Josephine's brother, to name their first-born. Reuben, aka "The Joker," decided that Bruce was a nice name, so he decided to name me Bruce Bruce. I have gone by my middle name — David — ever since.

Being named Bruce David Bruce hasn't been all bad. Bank tellers remember me very quickly, so I don't often have to show an ID. It can be fun in charades, also. When I was a counselor as a teenager at Camp Echoing Hills in Warsaw, Ohio, a fellow counselor gave the signs for "sounds like" and "two words," then she pointed to a bruise on her leg twice. Bruise Bruise? Oh yeah, Bruce Bruce is the answer!

Uncle Reuben, by the way, gave me a haircut when I was in kindergarten. He cut my hair short and shaved a small bald spot on the back of my head. My mother wouldn't let me go to school until the bald spot grew out again.

Of all my brothers and sisters (six in all), I am the only transplant to Athens, Ohio. I was born in Newark, Ohio, and have lived all around Southeastern Ohio. However, I moved to Athens to go to Ohio University and have never left.

At Ohio U, I never could make up my mind whether to major in English or Philosophy, so I got a bachelor's degree with a double major in both areas, then I added a Master of Arts degree in English and a Master of Arts degree in Philosophy. Yes, I have my MAMA degree.

Currently, and for a long time to come (I eat fruits and veggies), I am spending my retirement writing books such as *Nadia Comaneci: Perfect 10*, *The Funniest People in Dance*, *Homer's* Iliad: *A Retelling in Prose*, and *William Shakespeare's* Othello: *A Retelling in Prose*.

By the way, my sister Brenda Kennedy writes romances such as *A New Beginning* and *Shattered Dreams*.

# APPENDIX C: SOME BOOKS BY DAVID BRUCE

**Retellings of a Classic Work of Literature**

*Arden of Faversham: A Retelling*

*Ben Jonson's* The Alchemist: *A Retelling*

*Ben Jonson's* The Arraignment, or Poetaster: *A Retelling*

*Ben Jonson's* Bartholomew Fair: *A Retelling*

*Ben Jonson's* The Case is Altered: *A Retelling*

*Ben Jonson's* Catiline's Conspiracy: *A Retelling*

*Ben Jonson's* The Devil is an Ass: *A Retelling*

*Ben Jonson's* Epicene: *A Retelling*

*Ben Jonson's* Every Man in His Humor: *A Retelling*

*Ben Jonson's* Every Man Out of His Humor: *A Retelling*

*Ben Jonson's* The Fountain of Self-Love, or Cynthia's Revels: *A Retelling*

*Ben Jonson's* The Magnetic Lady, or Humors Reconciled: *A Retelling*

*Ben Jonson's* The New Inn, or The Light Heart: *A Retelling*

*Ben Jonson's* Sejanus' Fall: *A Retelling*

*Ben Jonson's* The Staple of News: *A Retelling*

*Ben Jonson's* A Tale of a Tub: *A Retelling*

*Ben Jonson's* Volpone, or the Fox: *A Retelling*

*Christopher Marlowe's Complete Plays: Retellings*

*Christopher Marlowe's* Dido, Queen of Carthage: *A Retelling*

*Christopher Marlowe's* Doctor Faustus: *Retellings of the 1604 A-Text and of the 1616 B-Text*

*Christopher Marlowe's* Edward II: *A Retelling*

*Christopher Marlowe's* The Massacre at Paris: *A Retelling*

*Christopher Marlowe's* The Rich Jew of Malta: *A Retelling*

*Christopher Marlowe's* Tamburlaine, Parts 1 and 2: *Retellings*

*Dante's* Divine Comedy: *A Retelling in Prose*

*Dante's* Inferno: *A Retelling in Prose*

*Dante's* Purgatory: *A Retelling in Prose*

*Dante's* Paradise: *A Retelling in Prose*

The Famous Victories of Henry V: *A Retelling*

*From the* Iliad *to the* Odyssey: *A Retelling in Prose of Quintus of Smyrna's* Posthomerica

*George Chapman, Ben Jonson, and John Marston's* Eastward Ho! *A Retelling*

*George Peele's* The Arraignment of Paris: *A Retelling*
*George Peele's* The Battle of Alcazar: *A Retelling*
*George Peele's* David and Bathsheba, and the Tragedy of Absalom: *A Retelling*
*George Peele's* Edward I: *A Retelling*
*George Peele's* The Old Wives' Tale: *A Retelling*
George-a-Greene: *A Retelling*
The History of King Leir: *A Retelling*
*Homer's* Iliad: *A Retelling in Prose*
*Homer's* Odyssey: *A Retelling in Prose*
*J.W. Gent.'s* The Valiant Scot: *A Retelling*
*Jason and the Argonauts: A Retelling in Prose of Apollonius of Rhodes'* Argonautica
*John Ford: Eight Plays Translated into Modern English*
*John Ford's* The Broken Heart: *A Retelling*
*John Ford's* The Fancies, Chaste and Noble: *A Retelling*
*John Ford's* The Lady's Trial: *A Retelling*
*John Ford's* The Lover's Melancholy: *A Retelling*
*John Ford's* Love's Sacrifice: *A Retelling*
*John Ford's* Perkin Warbeck: *A Retelling*
*John Ford's* The Queen: *A Retelling*
*John Ford's* 'Tis Pity She's a Whore: *A Retelling*
*John Lyly's* Campaspe: *A Retelling*
*John Lyly's* Endymion, The Man in the Moon: *A Retelling*
*John Lyly's* Galatea: *A Retelling*
*John Lyly's* Love's Metamorphosis: *A Retelling*
*John Lyly's* Midas: *A Retelling*
*John Lyly's* Mother Bombie: *A Retelling*
*John Lyly's* Sappho and Phao: *A Retelling*
*John Lyly's* The Woman in the Moon: *A Retelling*
*John Webster's* The White Devil: *A Retelling*
King Edward III: *A Retelling*
Mankind: *A Medieval Morality Play* (A Retelling)
*Margaret Cavendish's* The Unnatural Tragedy: *A Retelling*
The Merry Devil of Edmonton: *A Retelling*
The Summoning of Everyman: *A Medieval Morality Play* (A Retelling)
*Robert Greene's* Friar Bacon and Friar Bungay: *A Retelling*
The Taming of a Shrew: *A Retelling*
*Tarlton's Jests: A Retelling*
*Thomas Middleton's* A Chaste Maid in Cheapside: *A Retelling*
*Thomas Middleton's* Women Beware Women: *A Retelling*

*Thomas Middleton and Thomas Dekker's* The Roaring Girl: *A Retelling*

*Thomas Middleton and William Rowley's* The Changeling: *A Retelling*

*The Trojan War and Its Aftermath: Four Ancient Epic Poems*

*Virgil's* Aeneid: *A Retelling in Prose*

*William Shakespeare's 5 Late Romances: Retellings in Prose*

*William Shakespeare's 10 Histories: Retellings in Prose*

*William Shakespeare's 11 Tragedies: Retellings in Prose*

*William Shakespeare's 12 Comedies: Retellings in Prose*

*William Shakespeare's 38 Plays: Retellings in Prose*

*William Shakespeare's* 1 Henry IV, aka Henry IV, Part 1: *A Retelling in Prose*

*William Shakespeare's* 2 Henry IV, aka Henry IV, Part 2: *A Retelling in Prose*

*William Shakespeare's* 1 Henry VI, aka Henry VI, Part 1: *A Retelling in Prose*

*William Shakespeare's* 2 Henry VI, aka Henry VI, Part 2: *A Retelling in Prose*

*William Shakespeare's* 3 Henry VI, aka Henry VI, Part 3: *A Retelling in Prose*

*William Shakespeare's* All's Well that Ends Well: *A Retelling in Prose*

*William Shakespeare's* Antony and Cleopatra: *A Retelling in Prose*

*William Shakespeare's* As You Like It: *A Retelling in Prose*

*William Shakespeare's* The Comedy of Errors: *A Retelling in Prose*

*William Shakespeare's* Coriolanus: *A Retelling in Prose*

*William Shakespeare's* Cymbeline: *A Retelling in Prose*

*William Shakespeare's* Hamlet: *A Retelling in Prose*

*William Shakespeare's* Henry V: *A Retelling in Prose*

*William Shakespeare's* Henry VIII: *A Retelling in Prose*

*William Shakespeare's* Julius Caesar: *A Retelling in Prose*

*William Shakespeare's* King John: *A Retelling in Prose*

*William Shakespeare's* King Lear: *A Retelling in Prose*

*William Shakespeare's* Love's Labor's Lost: *A Retelling in Prose*

*William Shakespeare's* Macbeth: *A Retelling in Prose*

*William Shakespeare's* Measure for Measure: *A Retelling in Prose*

*William Shakespeare's* The Merchant of Venice: *A Retelling in Prose*

*William Shakespeare's* The Merry Wives of Windsor: *A Retelling in Prose*

*William Shakespeare's* A Midsummer Night's Dream: *A Retelling in Prose*

*William Shakespeare's* Much Ado About Nothing: *A Retelling in Prose*

*William Shakespeare's* Othello: *A Retelling in Prose*

*William Shakespeare's* Pericles, Prince of Tyre: *A Retelling in Prose*

*William Shakespeare's* Richard II: *A Retelling in Prose*

*William Shakespeare's* Richard III: *A Retelling in Prose*

*William Shakespeare's* Romeo and Juliet: *A Retelling in Prose*

*William Shakespeare's* The Taming of the Shrew: *A Retelling in Prose*

*William Shakespeare's* The Tempest: *A Retelling in Prose*
*William Shakespeare's* Timon of Athens: *A Retelling in Prose*
*William Shakespeare's* Titus Andronicus: *A Retelling in Prose*
*William Shakespeare's* Troilus and Cressida: *A Retelling in Prose*
*William Shakespeare's* Twelfth Night: *A Retelling in Prose*
*William Shakespeare's* The Two Gentlemen of Verona: *A Retelling in Prose*
*William Shakespeare's* The Two Noble Kinsmen: *A Retelling in Prose*
*William Shakespeare's* The Winter's Tale: *A Retelling in Prose*